GATE
OF THE
GODS

Other books by Thurman C. Petty, Jr.:

The Temple Gates:
Josiah Purges Judah's Idolatry

Siege at the Eastern Gate:
The Story of Hezeziah and Sennacherib

Fire in the Gates:
The Drama of Jeremiah and the Fall of Judah

The Open Gates:
From Babylon's Ashes, Freedom for the Jews

To order,
call
1-800-765-6955.

Visit us at
www.reviewandherald.com
for information on other Review and Herald® products.

GATE
OF THE
GODS

God's Quest for Nebuchadnezzar

THURMAN C. PETTY, JR.

Autumn
House® Publishing
www.autumnhousepublishing.com
A Division of **REVIEW AND HERALD® PUBLISHING**
Since 1861

Published by Autumn House® Publishing, a division of Review and Herald®
Publishing, Hagerstown, MD 21741-1119

Autumn House® titles may be purchased in bulk for educational, business, fund-rais-
ing, or sales promotional use. For information, please e-mail
SpecialMarkets@reviewandherald.com.

Autumn House® Publishing publishes biblically based materials for spiritual, physical,
and mental growth and Christian discipleship.

The author assumes full responsibility for the accuracy of all facts and quotations as
cited in this book.

Unless otherwise noted, Bible texts in this book are from the *Holy Bible, New
International Version.* Copyright © 1973, 1978, 1984, International Bible Society. Used
by permission of Zondervan Bible Publishers.

This book was
Edited by Gerald Wheeler
Designed by Trent Truman
Cover art by Thiago Lobo
Typeset: Bembo 11.5/13.5

PRINTED IN U.S.A.

12 11 10 09 08   5 4 3 2 1

Library of Congress Cataloging-in-Publication Data
Petty, Thurman C., 1940-   .
    Gate of the gods : God's quest for Nebuchadnezzar / Thurman C. Petty, Jr.
        p. cm.
    1. Nebuchadnezzar II, King of Babylonia, d. 562 B.C.—Fiction. 2. Bible. O.T.—
History of Biblical events—Fiction. 3. Iraq—History—To 634—Fiction. 4. Kings
and rulers—Fiction. 5. Babylonia—Fiction. 6. Religious fiction. I. Title.
    PS3566.E894G38 2007
    813'.54—dc22

                                    2007029175

ISBN 978-0-8127-0444-0

Dedication

To Jesus
who is the True Gate to God

Contents

CHAPTER 1 Evil Tidings From the North 13

CHAPTER 2 Gate of the Gods 30

CHAPTER 3 Conflict .42

CHAPTER 4 "Rising Star" 55

CHAPTER 5 Dream of Destiny 61

CHAPTER 6 A Donkey Brays His Last . . . . ,71

CHAPTER 7 Trial by Fire 79

CHAPTER 8 Almost Persuaded 90

CHAPTER 9 Crushing the Revolt 97

CHAPTER 10 Cut Down the Tree 113

ANCIENT BABYLON (Artist's conception)—This painting by J. Bardin shows the Ishtar Gate (center), covered with blue-glazed bricks. Procession Street passed through the gate, connecting important temples and palaces of the city, and was the scene of many colorful processions. The Hanging Gardens of Babylon (upper right) form part of the palace area. In the background stands the seven-staged temple tower (Etemenanki) in Marduk's great temple compound known as E-sagila. (Photo courtesy of Oriental Institute, University of Chicago.)

A Chronology of the Time of Daniel and Nebuchadnezzar

Years BC	Babylon	Judah	Prophets	Major Events
607			Jeremiah	
606				
605				Battle of Carchemish/Jerusalem: First Captivity
604				
603		Jehoiakim		
602			Daniel	(?) Nebuchadnezzar's Image Dream (Dan. 2)
601				
600				
599				
598				
597		Jehoiachin - 3 months		Jerusalem: Second Captivity
596				
595				
594	Nebuchadnezzar		=	(?) Golden Image/Fiery Furnace (Dan. 3)
593			=	Ezekiel's Vision of God (Eze. 1)
592				Elders With Ezekiel (Eze. 8:1)
591		Zedekiah		Ezekiel Rebukes Elders (Eze. 20:1)
590				
589				(?) Obadiah's Ministry
588				Jerusalem Siege Begins
587			Ezekiel	Siege of Tyre Begins (lasts 13 years)
586				Jerusalem Destroyed
585				Exiles in Babylon Hear of Fall of Jerusalem
584				
583				
582			=*	
581			=	
580				
579				
578				
577				
576				
575				Fall of Tyre
574				
573				
572				(?) Nebuchadnezzar's Madness Begins
571				
570				
569			=*	Eclipse
568			=	
567				
566				
565				(?) Nebuchadnezzar's Last Dream About God (Dan. 4)
564				
563				
562				
561	Amel Marduk			
560				

*Ending dates of prophets' ministries not known.

9

Jerusalem in the Time of Jeremiah

(Compiled from several maps by Thurman C. Petty, Jr.)

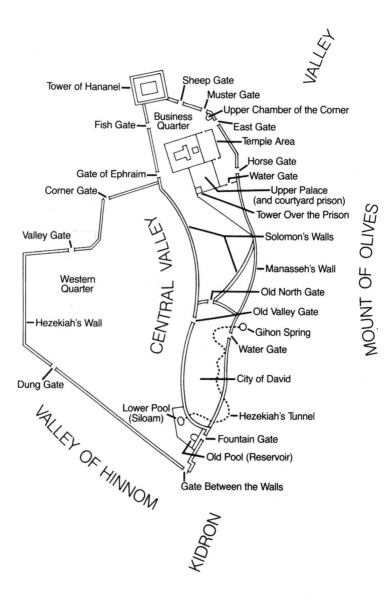

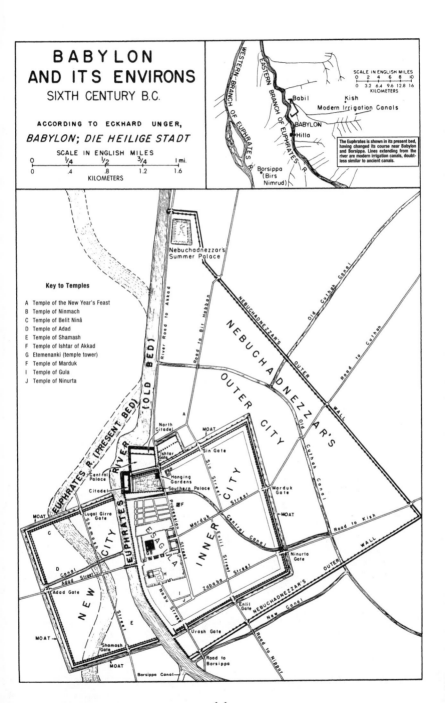

BABYLON
AND ITS ENVIRONS
SIXTH CENTURY B.C.

ACCORDING TO ECKHARD UNGER,

BABYLON; DIE HEILIGE STADT

SCALE IN ENGLISH MILES

0	1/4	1/2	3/4	1 mi.
0	.4	.8	1.2	1.6

KILOMETERS

SCALE IN ENGLISH MILES
0 2 4 6 8 10
0 3.2 6.4 9.6 12.8 16
KILOMETERS

WESTERN BRANCH OF EUPHRATES R.

EASTERN BRANCH OF EUPHRATES R.

Babil   Kish
Modern Irrigation Canals

BABYLON
Hilla

Borsippa
(Birs
Nimrud)

The Euphrates is shown in its present bed, having changed its course near Babylon and Borsippa. Lines extending from the river are modern irrigation canals, doubtless similar to ancient canals.

Key to Temples

A Temple of the New Year's Feast
B Temple of Ninmach
C Temple of Belit Ninâ
D Temple of Adad
E Temple of Shamash
F Temple of Ishtar of Akkad
G Etemenanki (temple tower)
F Temple of Marduk
I Temple of Gula
J Temple of Ninurta

Nebuchadnezzar's
Summer Palace

River Road to Akkad

Road to Bil Habban

NEBUCHADNEZZAR'S

Old Cuthah Canal

Road to Cuthah

NEBUCHADNEZZAR'S OUTER

Old Cuthah Canal

OUTER CITY

OUTER WALL

North
Citadel   MOAT

Ishtar
Gate   Sin Gate

Central
Palace   Sin Street

Citadel   Hanging
Gardens
Southern Palace

MOAT   Lugal Girra
Gate

INNER CITY

Marduk
Gate

MOAT

EUPHRATES R. (OLD BED)

EUPHRATES R. (PRESENT BED)

Procession Street

ESAGILA

F

Marduk Street

Central Canal

Road to Kish

C

Canal
Adad Street

D

Adad Gate

NEW CITY

Nabu Street

Enlil Street

Zababa Street

G H
A
J

Ninurta
Gate

OUTER WALL

MOAT

E

Shamash
Gate

MOAT

Urash Gate

Enlil
Gate   NEBUCHADNEZZAR'S

New Canal

Road to Nippur

Road to Borsippa

Road to
Borsippa

Borsippa Canal

Chapter 1

Evil Tidings
From the North

Nebuchadnezzar couldn't have been more pleased with himself. Though only 18, he commanded his ailing father's principal army and had just destroyed a fortress held by one of the most powerful nations in the world. Now its survivors fled home.

"I want my best troops to dog the Egyptians' tail." The crown prince leaned over the railing of his battle chariot and shouted the order to a nearby messenger. "Tell them to press the enemy hard. Don't let a single man get away."

The courier urged his horse after the Babylonian forces pursuing the retreating enemy. As he passed fellow Babylonian soldiers, he occasionally sent a man sprawling to the ground. No matter. He deemed Nebuchadnezzar's orders more important than the comforts of ordinary soldiers. The steed climbed the hill south of Carchemish, gingerly at first while dodging the corpses that littered the road, and then spreading its legs for speed as it gained the summit. In minutes it overtook the commander of the forward platoons.

Nebuchadnezzar smiled as in the distance he saw the messenger rein up before one of his under officers. He fancied that his message would spur the tired men to new strength—to push forward on an offensive urged by their commander in chief. In fact, the troops would fight for the young general until they dropped, because many hoped that one day he would be their king.

"Head on up the hill," Nebuchadnezzar barked to his driver. "I want to keep up with the front."

The crown prince hailed another messenger. "Have my officers hold the bulk of my army in reserve," he called. "We need to ensure the loyalty of all the cities as we advance toward Egypt."

Nebuchadnezzar glanced back at Carchemish as his chariot headed south toward Hamath. The city behind him lay in ruins. Pharaoh Necho II had captured it four years earlier, and had used it as a base from which to harass Babylon. He had wanted to save what was left of the dying Assyrian empire, preserving it as a buffer between the Nile and the growing power of Babylon.

But now Egypt had been punished. A squadron of Babylonian military engineers had already begun organizing the surviving townspeople of Carchemish to rebuild its walls and towers.

Carchemish guarded an important ford. The Euphrates River flowed along its eastern wall so shallow at this point that people could wade across. Egypt and Babylon both knew that whoever held Carchemish controlled the crossing and all the fabulous trade that passed through the region.

And now Babylon guarded the ford. Its only serious rival had fled south through Palestine, seeking to reach Egyptian soil before total ruin overtook it.

The Babylonian crown prince surveyed the battlefield littered with thousands of dead and dying, scattered as far as the eye could see. His heart ached at the loss of so many brave men. Many homes would never again know the laughter of fathers, brothers, and sons. *Shouldn't there be a better way to settle international problems?* he wondered. No. He answered his own question. Not as long as other nations harassed Babylon, or resisted his father's desire to control world trade. *When every nation rests under Babylon's umbrella,* he thought, *then war and suffering will cease. I'll see to that.*

Nebuchadnezzar's mind snapped to the present as a mounted messenger drew up alongside his moving chariot. "Your elite forces press the enemy, my lord," he called, "and your generals have halted the main army as you ordered. They're taking their midday rest, and await further instructions."

"Pull up by those trees." The young commander pointed as he spoke to his driver, nodding to the messenger to follow. Scanning ahead, he eyed the last Egyptian stragglers in the distance, his soldiers in pursuit. Around him, using whatever shade they could find, his main army enjoyed their customary midday rest, nibbling on bread, sipping wine, and joking—relieved to have survived a major battle.

"Summon my generals." The crown prince issued the order as he stepped down from his chariot, while his servants scurried to erect a shelter under a nearby tree.

No one can stop me now, he thought, flushed with victory. *I control all Hatti-land,[1] from Lebanon to Egypt. Soon the fabulous wealth of these fertile nations will be mine. Someday I shall be king of Babylon, and this will be the gem of my crown.*

❧

The ominous retreat of Egypt launched dark rumors throughout Judah. Its royal messenger service scurried day and night, reporting the position of the approaching Babylonians to the king.

The city of Babylon actually lay far to the east, but inhospitable deserts made a direct crossing impractical. So most people traveling from Babylon to Palestine followed the Euphrates River northwest to Carchemish, and then turned southward through the fertile valleys of Syria, Lebanon, and

Israel—a total distance of nearly 1,000 miles. Thus the Babylonians approached Judah from the north, as had most of Judah's enemies throughout its history.

Babylonian advance forces harried the Egyptian stragglers as they hurried past Jerusalem. Bone-weary soldiers of the Nile, desperate for life, often met an unceremonious death at the hands of their pursuers. Some fell from exhaustion and expired without a good-night kiss from an enemy sword. Soon all living participants disappeared in the southwest, leaving hundreds of carcasses along the road. Judahite scouts patrolled the roads between Jerusalem and the Great Sea (the Mediterranean), ready to warn of the approach of hostile forces.

Royal messengers brought the reassuring news that the main enemy force had occupied itself besieging towns and cities in Lebanon and Syria. Nebuchadnezzar had a score to settle with the governor of Phoenicia and Syria, for he had rebelled against Babylon and allied with Egypt.

Jehoiakim had no doubts about Babylon's intentions. Now in his third year of rule, the Judahite king had been placed upon his throne by Pharaoh Necho II of Egypt, who had killed his father, Josiah, in battle. His brother Jehoahaz had reigned for a short time, but Necho had had him taken to Egypt in chains. For this, Jehoiakim was thankful, for his brother's misfortune had given him the crown.

Now his own luck had faded. Jehoiakim's loyalty to Egypt had become well known, and had brought him special favors. But Babylon had now defeated the empire of the Nile, and where did that leave him? How would he rate at the hands of an army that had decimated his allies?

Talons of fear slipped slowly around his throat, tightening their grip with every new update on enemy movements. A fist-sized rock weighed down his stomach, and his temples ached with pressure from an unseen vise that slowly squashed his brain.

Panic pushed Jehoiakim to the brink of desperation. He had never been a patient man, and those near him feared his violent temper. He had been known to whip out his sword and kill those who dared offend him. Now every official and servant sought some excuse to work elsewhere, away from the murderous rage of this caged lion of Judah.

"Where are my counselors?" he roared at a hapless attendant who brought refreshments to him.

"I-I don't know, Y-your Majesty," he stammered.

"Well, find them, you worthless rat. They've got work to do."

The household servant-turned-messenger hurried in search of the counselors. Enlisting the aid of a palace guard, he sent first one and then others heading toward the throne room. Soon the fate of Judah would be decided, and nothing would ever be the same again.

"I've never seen anything like it, Daniel," gasped a tall man in the long, form-fitting linen garment of a priest. He stroked his graying hair and gawked at the stragglers from Pharaoh's army as they fled south. "The Egyptian army seldom fears any foe," he mused. "They must have met with a disastrous defeat."

"Yes, Jeremiah, sir," replied the 18-year-old young man as he leaned over the battlements of Jerusalem. "They must be really afraid, coming so far up in the highlands here instead of taking the easier and more direct coastal road back to Egypt."

The two stood silently watching the weary soldiers skirting the ancient city. Many seemed to have abandoned their weapons long before reaching Jerusalem.

Jeremiah and Daniel descended the stairs of the tower and went their separate ways. Each recognized that Babylon bore down on Judah from the north, and that life as they had known it would soon change. Egypt no longer stood as protector to their tiny but wealthy nation, and Judah now lay helpless before the greed of any strong army seeking conquest.

Daniel hurried to his home that lay near the palace, just south of the Temple. Quiet, but with a transparent inner strength, he always displayed a slight smile that easily broadened into an irresistible grin. His eyes often flashed a twinkle that softened their steady gaze. The color of one iris seemed of a lighter hue than the other, and slightly larger.

Daniel stood at average height, but most would have thought him taller. Moving with the easy grace of a trained dancer, he belonged to the Jewish royal family.

After Daniel's grandfather Josiah had died, his uncle Eliakim had become king. Pharaoh had changed his name to Jehoiakim. Daniel belonged to the family of Jehoiakim's brother Mataniah (soon to become Zedekiah). The young man did not stand in line for the throne, but he still ranked high in Judah's social structure.

As he passed the East Gate he heard a familiar voice behind him.

"Daniel, wait!"

Turning, he saw three of his cousins hurrying up the street behind him. "Hananiah!" He smiled at the older boy as the trio encircled him. "Have you finished your lessons so soon?"

"No," the other panted. "Our teacher sent us home. He didn't think it safe in the Temple with the Egyptian army so near. Who knows what those desperate men might do?"

"Don't worry, Hananiah," Daniel said, laughing. He pointed to the huge cedar doors just behind him. "The gates are shut and barred. It would take a major siege to break into Jerusalem."

"You're right," his cousin Mishael agreed. "But you know the Temple scribe. He fears his own shadow at times."

"He does at that," Azariah, the youngest, added. Though tallest of the three, he had little flesh on his limbs. Though somewhat awkward, he had a ready grin that showed his immaculate teeth through a stubby beard. "But he makes our lessons interesting." Azariah always had a good word to say about everyone.

"Let's get out of here," Daniel urged. "I don't like the smell of this place." He glanced at the poorly covered sewage channel that ran along the edge of East Street and through the gate.

The quartet ambled down the street that paralleled the wall south of the Potsherd Gate.[2] They discussed the Egyptian rout, the apparent strength of Babylon, and the fear that gripped Jerusalem; then at his home Daniel split off from the trio.

"Be careful," he called from the door of his house. "Trust in Yahweh,[3] and He will take care of you. *Shalom alekim* ["Peace be with you"]!" He fastened the door, glanced at the animal pens that occupied the first floor, and ascended the stairs to the living quarters.

Though some would have called Daniel's home a palace, it was smaller and simpler than many owned by Judahite nobles. Spacious, decorated with flower designs on the white plaster walls, it was a marked contrast to the gray-walled hovels of most citizens of Jerusalem.

"Ah, Daniel." His mother looked up from the pot of vegetable stew bubbling on the brazier in the cooking area. "It's nearly time for the noon meal, and your father is ready for family prayer."

"Yes, Mother. We need Yahweh's blessing now more than ever before."

"Oh?" She searched her son's face.

"Who knows what will happen to us when Babylon reaches Jerusalem."

"How true." She ladled the stew into a large pottery bowl and placed a dish of dried fruit beside it. Then she beckoned to the other family members.

❧❧❧

"Will the Babylonians really come here?" Daniel asked during one of their classes in an anteroom of the Temple.

"Yes," Jeremiah, his teacher, answered. King Jehoiakim hated the prophet, and didn't know that he taught the young men, for he left such "insignificant details" to the priests and Levites.

"But we're God's chosen people," Mishael protested. "Shouldn't He protect us?"

"We are His people, Mishael." Jeremiah gazed through a window at the sanctuary, now in shameful disrepair. "But most Jews have forgotten Him, and would rather do evil than good."

"But didn't Grandfather Josiah lead Israel back to God?" Daniel questioned. "He destroyed pagan shrines throughout the land."

"Josiah tried," Jeremiah said with a sigh, "but he couldn't force the people to return to God. They obeyed the king, but in their hearts they remained as pagan as before he launched his reforms.

"Look at the high places they've rebuilt around Jerusalem." The prophet swept his hand in a wide arc, pointing toward prominent places around the city.

"On every rooftop and hill, people offer cakes to Ashtoreth—'the queen of heaven.'" He spat out the window in disgust. "And the Mount of Olives has many pagan shrines along its southern slope—in full view of the Temple! Solomon himself started that outrage, and not even Josiah could stop it." The prophet paced the floor, fists on hips, jaw set in anger, but with tears collecting at the corners of his eyes.

Daniel knew that his teacher mourned for the apostasy of Israel, and that nothing short of total revival could satisfy his inner yearning to reconcile his people with God. "What will happen to us?" asked the young prince. "Where will it end?"

Pausing in his pacing, Jeremiah eyed his brightest pupil. He opened his mouth to speak, but closed it again and gazed out at the Temple for several minutes.

"Jerusalem will die, Daniel," he murmured at last as he slid his foot back and forth on the stone pavement. "Yahweh will bring His servant Nebuchadnezzar from the north to destroy Judah and deport our people."

"Why don't you tell the people about all this?" Hananiah demanded.

"I have. I've preached it for years, and nobody listens."

"My father said they tried to stone you in the Temple," Azariah commented. "They'd have killed you if Ahikim and the other princes hadn't stopped them."

"But can't you do something?" Mishael insisted.

"I've thought of writing God's messages down in a scroll," the prophet answered. "But what good that will do, I have no idea."

❧

Nebuchadnezzar took his time moving south from Carchemish. His vast army had received a large influx of reserves from Babylon, and the crown prince advanced on Hamath, where once again he grappled with remnants of the Egyptian army. But Babylon won the day again, and Pharaoh's troops continued their desperate flight.

Passing through Syria, Nebuchadnezzar besieged every city that refused Babylonian control, sending thousands east to Babylon in chains. Many cities put up only token resistance, for the bloodthirsty tactics of all Mesopotamian conquerors had become well known through the centuries. Few wanted to arouse Nebuchadnezzar's fury, for that would be suicide.

King Jehoiakim of Judah cringed at the thought of so cruel an enemy entering his capital city, and decided at first to resist. "The Babylonians could never capture Jerusalem," he boasted. "We have impregnable walls, and the best defenders in the world. Nebuchadnezzar would be foolish to waste his army fighting me."

But when the Chaldean hordes cascaded over the northern hills and valleys above Jerusalem, the Judahite king changed his mind. "They'll crush us!" he exclaimed, as he watched tens of thousands of battle-seasoned veterans systematically surround his city like ants ready to harvest a pool of honey. He visualized his own capture and execution at their merciless hands.

Nebuchadnezzar assigned a sizable force to besiege Jerusalem while he continued south toward Egypt. His elite battalions quickly neutralized all resistance, and the crown prince faced little opposition. Within a few days he stood before Pelusium on the borders of Egypt, prepared for the final thrust. Victory over Necho II seemed within his grasp.

The young Babylonian commander had not yet engaged Pharaoh when a messenger arrived bearing Jehoiakim's surrender note: "Spare our lives," the Judahite king pleaded. "We will be your slaves."

"Good!" laughed the young prince as his scribe finished reading the document. "They'll pay more taxes alive than dead. Take a message for Jerusalem."

The scribe held his writing tools at the ready—a reed brush and a broken piece of pottery that he would use to take notes down on.

"I accept your surrender," the crown prince dictated. "No one will die unless you resist me. I will expect to receive hostages as a guarantee of your loyalty."

Later the scribe would copy the message on a tablet of soft

clay, incising it in cuneiform—intricate patterns of wedge-shaped characters. He worked quickly, but with great care, for his commander's message must not be misunderstood.

He had not yet finished when a courier galloped up, dismounted, and threw himself at Nebuchadnezzar's feet. "My lord," he panted. "The great king, King Nabopolassar of Babylon, has died, and your brothers are discussing who should take the crown!"

"My brothers!" the young prince stormed as he stomped down the steps of his portable throne. "Those traitors! They know that Father chose me." He turned, staring toward Egypt for a moment, tears pooling in the corners of his eyes as he remembered his father. "He's dead," he mumbled. "The famous conqueror of Nineveh—the one who ended the tyranny of Assyria. I'll never see him again."

Pushing aside his grief, Nebuchadnezzar launched into action. "General!" he shouted. From somewhere behind him a royal officer bowed himself into Nebuchadnezzar's presence. "I'm going to Babylon to secure the throne. Take charge here."

"Yes, my lord," said the general, smiling. He was grateful for such good fortune. His stars must have designated glory for his future, for now he directly commanded Babylon's greatest army.

"Jerusalem has surrendered," Nebuchadnezzar told him, "and I have promised to spare the people unless they resist. Transfer the army there and see that the arrangements have been properly concluded."

"How many hostages will you want, my lord?" The general straightened up.

"Ten thousand. From among the princes, craftsmen, officials, scribes. Don't drain the city, of course, but bring me the best." Nebuchadnezzar paused as he considered his plans. "Treat them well, for they may be useful to me."

"When will you leave, my lord?"

"Within the hour." Nebuchadnezzar turned, then paused. "We'll have to forget Egypt for now, so when you're finished in Jerusalem, bring the army to Babylon. If my brothers give me any trouble, I may need you. If not—well, the troops have fought long enough for this year."

"May the gods favor you, my lord," the general said as he bowed his leave.

✿✿

The news of Jehoiakim's surrender rippled throughout Jerusalem, spreading terror. Thousands fled the city or hid in caves or anywhere that might offer refuge from the bloodlust of a victorious army. Kings did not pay their armies much. Soldiers hoped to gain some wealth from pillaging conquered cities and towns.

"Why did Jehoiakim surrender?" Mishael protested. The three cousins had joined Daniel's family in the food-storage chamber beneath their house. Pearls of sweat glistened on his high forehead and dripped off his nose. "Doesn't he know they massacre their captives?"

"And rape women, and skin people alive, and steal everything of value," added Hananiah. "Yes, Mishael, he knows."

The sound of a ram's-horn trumpet echoed from afar, signaling the order to open the gates.

"Don't be afraid." Daniel had not lost his smile. Even amid the crisis he remained at peace with himself and with God. "Remember what Jeremiah taught us? God says, 'Those who honor me I will honor.'"[4]

"You're right, Daniel." Hananiah sighed as he scratched at his stubble beard. "Our parents taught us to trust Him always. I guess now's the time we need to follow their counsel."

Daniel motioned for silence. "Let's agree among ourselves, and before God, that we will be true to Him—no matter what happens."

"Agreed," the others chorused.

The tension eased, and the family shared the promises they had learned from Scripture. Mishael managed to smile as he felt his muscles relax.

The guards at the East Gate unbarred their giant doors and started to open them. But when they saw the mass of Babylonian troops ready to spring through the opening, they fled, allowing the enemy to complete the job.

Fierce warriors poured into the city, ready for any foe. But they found the streets deserted, save for a few stray animals.

Undaunted, they searched from house to house. They knew all the likely hiding places, and soon filled the cobblestone avenues with people ousted from their homes. Guards lined them up so that their officers could select their hostages. Though gruff and arrogant, they injured no one, save those who resisted, but herded thousands to the city square just inside the East Gate to form them into traveling parties for the long trek to Babylon.

Daniel's family showed no surprise or resistance when two armed soldiers sprang into their cave and motioned for them to return to the surface. Shielding their eyes from the sun's glare, they stepped into the street, discovering that the Babylonians had already lined up all their neighbors.

"See what I told you?" Daniel whispered. "God has protected us. While they are looting the houses, they don't seem to be hurting anybody."

Jeremiah sadly watched from atop the northeast wall of the Temple as the bands of hostages started their long journey to Babylon. He saw among the captives some of the most promising young men of the city. A few had been allowed to take along their wives, but most would travel alone. The invaders had also selected an occasional beautiful woman to become a concubine of the king or some nobleman. The women would ride in oxen-drawn carts.

Just then Jeremiah spotted Daniel and the three cousins among the captives. Daniel's unusual intelligence, good looks, and fearless devotion to God would have made him a valued advisor to the Judahite throne. But now, it seemed, he would languish in a dungeon, or slave away his life in some Babylonian craft industry.

The prophet's eyes filled with tears at the thought of such injustice. "Why did you allow them to take Daniel?" he cried in prayer. "Most of the hostages are pagans. But Daniel—"

He wiped his eyes with the back of his hand and glanced at an unusual movement below him. His scalp began to tingle as he saw Babylonian soldiers stride through the Temple court. A priest tried to stop them, but they shoved him aside and barged into the sacred building. Moments later they emerged carrying armloads of gold and silver bowls.

Within hours the Chaldeans and their hostages disappeared toward the north. Jeremiah would never see Daniel or his friends again. And the Temple vessels would soon grace the shelves of a pagan shrine.

※※

"We'll take the desert route,"[5] Nebuchadnezzar shouted to his private guard as he mounted his chariot. "We should make the crossing in about three or four weeks."

"Yes, my lord," the general replied. "Be careful. Many have gotten lost in those arid wastes."

"I have a good guide, and the gods will be with us. We'll be all right."

"What about water?"

"The guide tells me we'll find watering holes every day. There are date trees at the oases to provide us with some extra food."

"May the gods smooth your way, my lord." The general resigned himself to the fact that he could not dissuade his prince from the dangerous journey. He bowed and stepped back to allow the party to proceed.

"Move out," Nebuchadnezzar ordered. He glanced around at his escort as the chariot lurched forward. He had selected his finest warriors—men of proven bravery and loyalty, who had shown repeatedly that they could survive under any circumstance. This small band would protect him against desert chieftains and give him a fighting edge in Babylon should he meet with resistance.

Leaving the army at Pelusium, the small force headed north along the Mediterranean Sea, past Gaza, and then northeast over the mountains of Judah. They passed just north of Jerusalem, crossed the Jordan River valley, and then headed northeast through Ammon and Kedar.

The horses loped along at a measured pace that allowed them to travel for hours without exhaustion. The men rode in tight formation, ready for any emergency—their swords belted to their sides, bows and arrows slung across their shoulders, and spears tied at the ready on their saddles or chariots.

Scouts ranged the road two or three miles ahead to warn of ambush from desert raiders. Others lingered about a half mile behind to prevent surprise attack from the rear.

The royal party passed an oasis every 10 or 12 hours. Each time, they watered and fed their horses, rested under the palms, and ate what dates or other food they could find. They had wanted their stops to coincide with night, but things didn't always work out that way.

Nebuchadnezzar agonized over his plight as he rode

along. He had regained control of Palestine and decimated the Egyptian army, chasing the mighty pharaoh to his lair, ready to deal the deathblow that would place Egypt under Babylon's power. But it had all been for nothing.

His thoughts stumbled over one another. Grief over his father's death mingled with his frustration over the unfinished Egyptian campaign and his anger about his brothers' apparent treachery.

Three weeks later the weary brigade reached the fertile plain of Mesopotamia near a bend in the Euphrates River at Anat. Though exhausted, they forged on toward Babylon. The scouts stiffened their vigil, for a surprise attack now could lead to an early grave for the entire detachment.

Tension mounted as the royal party moved southeast. It had no time now for rest—speed offered the only hope for success. They used the less-frequented roads, hoping to conceal their presence until the last minute.

Babylon appeared on the horizon—beautiful, prosperous, sitting atop a mound of debris that had been 2,000 years in the making. The main temple tower rose majestically from its environs—"Etemenanki," long fabled as the original tower of Babel, now the temple of Babylon's main god, Marduk. City walls and buildings glinted in the harsh sunlight, their glazed brick surfaces glowing in blues, yellows, pinks, and reds. Still no opposition.

"We may make it yet." Nebuchadnezzar hesitated to relax with the prize almost within his grasp. "Careful of ambush at the gates. Courage, men! If we win the day, you will all be rewarded."

Weapons at the ready, they charged toward the open gates, shields ready to fend off the expected volley of arrows from the walls lining the road the last 200 feet. Nebuchadnezzar's banner fluttered from a spear held by the warrior at his right hand.

A trumpet sounded from the watchtower, and the riders tensed for battle, coaxing their horses for more speed. Just a few more yards . . . No enemy blocked the way . . . No incoming hail of arrows.

The trumpet repeated its call. Nebuchadnezzar, passing directly beneath the bugler's post, recognized the cadence.

"Halt!" he cried. "Stand still!"

The exhausted men obeyed without thinking, reigned in their horses, and awaited further orders. They glanced quickly from side to side, wary of imminent danger, nerves taut, ready to defend their crown prince.

"Advance in royal parade!" barked Nebuchadnezzar.

The dazed men complied, moving with measured pace along the grand Processional Way, while swarms of happy people spilled into the streets. The trumpet call had signaled the arrival of the king, and multitudes welcomed their new monarch to his capital city.

------

[1] Palestine and Syria.

[2] Another name for the East Gate. The area outside this gate had become a dumping ground for broken pottery.

[3] Yahweh is the personal name of God used frequently by Jeremiah and Ezekiel. It means "I AM," "the Eternal."

[4] 1 Samuel 2:30.

[5] A shortcut through the Arabian Desert—about 800 miles.

Chapter 2

Gate of the Gods

The joyous welcome Nebuchadnezzar received brought tears to his eyes. His father's death, the exhausting 800-mile journey, the mental strain, and now the sudden relief that his brothers had not stopped his entry into Babylon, all unnerved him—and yet filled him with jubilation. He pulled to the front of his men, raised his spear high over his head, and beamed down at his adoring subjects.

Men, women, and children stretched out to touch Nebuchadnezzar as he reined his horses from side to side. His sweaty hair and beard had become matted and stiff, his clothing covered with dust. Nothing in his appearance would excite any admiration. But the people saw more than a man. He was the heir, the next king of Babylon!

Nebuchadnezzar puzzled over the curious people who slowed his progress. They, too, wore dirty clothing. Many had shaved their hair and beards, while others had bloody gashes on their heads and arms. Most had sprinkled themselves with dust and ashes.

Ashes! Nebuchadnezzar's exhausted mind at last resolved the enigma—they too mourned the death of his father, their king.

With a wave of his spear, the crown prince turned toward the palace gate on the east side of the avenue. The doors stood open, and its courtyards overflowed with nobility gathered to welcome home their new leader.

Dressed in royal robes, Nebuchadnezzar stood in the south throne room of the palace. The huge hall—168 feet long by 57 feet wide—was the holy of holies for the government of Babylon. The glazed brick facade had a black background decorated with garlands of yellow and white palmettes, red and green columns topped by triple blue capitals, and all of it edged in gold. A contrasting horizontal band of lions enhanced the overall effect.

The nobles, courtiers, and bodyguards who surrounded Nebuchadnezzar seemed relieved that he had returned safely from the wars. They rejoiced that so able a son stood ready to assume leadership over the growing empire his father had founded.

The crown prince visually measured the men who supported his cause—officers of the court and the army, Chaldean nobles, and rulers from several conquered nations. Most of them would have been judged handsome by any standard, for rulers usually considered good looks and a strong physique among the most important traits for their high-ranking officials.

Although only 18 years of age, Nebuchadnezzar had already learned how to judge character and motives. Now he searched each face for any hostile intent. He still couldn't fathom why his brothers hadn't fought to gain the throne.

Could they still threaten me? he wondered. He eyed them as they joined with other officials and friends, encouraging his bid for control. *It doesn't make any sense,* he thought. *I'd have fought to the death for the crown. Perhaps the rumors about them were wrong.*

As they approached him he saw no malice, no jealousy in their eyes, no guile in their well-wishing. *I must reward them well,* he decided. *They saved the throne for me.*

His brothers had not stood alone in reserving the crown for Nebuchadnezzar. Several Chaldean nobles acted on instructions left by his father to discourage others from assuming control of the government. They risked their lives by publicly announcing that Nebuchadnezzar had been chosen successor.

In Babylon the royal coronation took place yearly on New Year's Day—Nisan 1 (April 22/23). But following a royal death, the people crowned a new king as soon as possible, and then reinstated him again every New Year's Day.

As the hour for coronation neared, the elegant parade of nobles and officials led the crown prince south on the Processional Way toward the "Esagila"—the sacred temple area. The street had been paved with bitumen—natural asphalt—while occasional bricks had been added for beauty. Many bricks bore the inscription of Sennacherib—the terrible king of Assyria in Hezekiah's time. On either side of the street, for 200 yards, ran a blue enameled mural with 60 multicolored lions on each side.

About a half mile south of the palace the line of nobles entered the courtyard of the famous tower of Babylon, which stood next to the temple of the chief Chaldean god, Marduk—often called Bel (lord of heaven and earth). Thousands of people crowded the enclosure, and other thousands filled nearby streets, craning their necks to glimpse their new king. Hundreds of priests milled through the crowd, each fulfilling his part of the service.

The spectators quieted when a small group began to climb the steps up the south slope of the 300-foot, seven-tiered tower. Two black-robed priests led the way. A nobleman followed them carrying the crown of Babylon, trailed by Nebuchadnezzar and then other priests and high officials.

The royal troop ascended slowly, stopping at intervals while the holy men chanted incantations. At the summit the nobles lined up on both sides while Nebuchadnezzar knelt before the high priest to receive his crown. The prelate lifted the bejeweled diadem, then set it upon the head of the young man bowed before him. In a loud voice he charged Nebuchadnezzar to uphold the integrity of his office, and then waved his hand over the new king.

Nebuchadnezzar rose to gaze at his city and its surrounding countryside. Actually a desert, when irrigated the area became a productive breadbasket. But only a strong central government could maintain the extensive canal system needed to ensure prosperity—a challenge for such a young man.

Nebuchadnezzar's gaze shifted to the metropolis nestled at his feet. Babylon, the golden city, the praise of the whole earth. Now it belonged to him. His eyes caressed the palace, the walls, the temples, the multitudes standing near the base of the tower. His heart stirred at the sight. *These people are depending on me,* he thought as the burden of leadership settled upon his shoulders. *They deserve the best I have to give. Yes,* he determined, *I vow to make this the greatest city on earth, and to rule these people with justice and respect.*

He turned again to face the priests and nobles. The high priest approached, chanting ritual phrases in an ancient tongue no longer understood by the common people. With great pomp he swung his hand in a wide arch, slapping Nebuchadnezzar broadside on the cheek with such force the new king nearly lost his balance. The blow smarted. Tears began to trickle down his cheeks.

The high priest examined Nebuchadnezzar's face, saw the tears, and smiled. Stepping to the edge of the landing, he cupped his hands and shouted: "The king weeps! Bel will be gracious to us in the coming year!"

Nebuchadnezzar smiled to himself as he wiped his face with a handkerchief. Descending the stairs, he crossed the giant courtyard to the temple of Marduk, where he worshipped the chief deity of the city. Then, emerging from the house of Bel, he raised his hands above his head and received the homage of his subjects. A great cheer rose from thousands of voices, and the people bowed before their new monarch, King Nebuchadnezzar of Babylon.

"It seems like a dream!" Nebuchadnezzar beamed at his chamberlain on the day after the coronation. The Chaldean officer had served King Nabopolassar and had seemed like a second father to the crown prince. "All during the hard ride across the desert, I imagined having to battle my brothers for the crown."

The chief of state bowed. "May my lord the king live forever." He recited the official greeting required of all. "They understood that your father named you. Besides, you're a warrior. Everyone knew that in a pitched battle you would win."

"Well, they acted wisely. See that they receive positions of honor." He fingered his elegant blue linen robe as he thought for a moment. "I also want to reward your own loyalty. And see that the other Chaldean regents receive rewards as well."

"Yes—thank you, my lord." The chamberlain turned to leave, but then stopped to look again at the handsome young king. "Will there be anything else, my lord?"

"Yes, lord chamberlain. I need to review my father's decrees, and I'd like to see his building plans."

Within minutes the royal architects assembled, carrying drawings of the projects proposed by the late king. Servants brought in a table, and Nebuchadnezzar bent over the plans for several hours.

"Your father, King Nabopolassar, asked us to remodel the temple tower," the chief architect explained, pointing to the detailed sketches. "We've made some progress already, but much still needs to be done."

"I noticed your work yesterday," Nebuchadnezzar said, "and I'm pleased with your craftsmanship. I like what I see here, too"—he waved his hand toward the drawings. "Finish all my father's buildings exactly as you've depicted them here."

The officials smiled to each other, for the king's approval of their plans would bring them many valuable contracts.

Nebuchadnezzar turned from the plans and seated himself on his throne, lost in thought for several minutes. *There's much more I'd like to do.* He paused and scratched his black beard. *The city has become crowded. Too many in such a small space. Causes problems in sanitation.* "We need to expand—perhaps add a new city across the river."

"A good idea, my lord," the chief architect nodded. "We'll put our designers to work on it right away."

"My wife, the Median princess Amuhia," the king continued, "grew up in the mountains, and she pines away for something that resembles home. But our flat plains have no mountains!" He raised his hands in mock exasperation, accompanied by a ripple of laughter from his courtiers. "Perhaps we could construct a large terraced building covered with trees, bushes, and flowers," he mused. "Maybe we can make our own mountain so that she'll feel at home with us."

The king's scribes pressed their square metal styli into moist clay tablets, recording all that the king said. They had no difficulty keeping up, for the king often paused to think through his ideas.

"All this construction will cost a lot of money." The young man scratched his head. "But then—" He paused again. "We're collecting ample booty from the wars. That should help. Babylon is the origin, the center of all lands, gentlemen—the navel of the world. We want to make this the greatest city of all, to bear witness to its living name: THE GATE OF THE GODS."

Gate of the Gods

Nebuchadnezzar worked with the architects into the evening, outlining other building projects. "The Ishtar Gate has become too small," he noted. "Lower the roadway and rebuild its foundations. Strengthen it with double walls. Redecorate the entire gate with a tiled frieze of oxen and dragons. Import cedar for the ceiling and the doors. Cover them with copper, and make the threshold and hinges of bronze. I want this gate to amaze everyone who enters the city. Oh, yes, inscribe each new brick with my name. I don't want anyone to forget what I've done to make this city the greatest on earth."

Within days of his coronation Nebuchadnezzar committed the charge of the city to his trusted officials, gathered his army about him, and marched off toward the northwest. He would now consolidate his victories in Syria and Palestine and collect the tribute and taxes he needed to finance his enormous building program.

Jerusalem had been brought to its knees. Little fighting took place, and few had died during the takeover. Yet the degradation of bowing to a pagan conqueror filled every man, woman, and child with grief. To show their deep despair, people roamed the streets wearing sackcloth and sprinkling their heads with ashes.

"Oh, the humiliation," Daniel's mother moaned as they waited in the street with others rounded up by their captors. "How can Yahweh let this happen, Daniel?" She turned to her handsome son, tears streaming down her face. "I gave you the name 'God is my judge' because I believed Yahweh defended His own against their enemies. But where is He now?"

"God is our judge, Mother." Daniel embraced her, moving slowly to avoid alarming their Babylonian guards. "He will care for us. But you know that Israel has forsaken

Yahweh. The prophets warned us that this would happen. We may suffer many indignities because of our nation's sins. But Yahweh will bless all who trust in Him."

"You're right, my son. I'm sorr—"

"You!" A Babylonian officer grabbed Daniel's arm, yanking him toward the East Gate. "You too," he bellowed at Hananiah, "and you, and you," he said, pointing at Mishael and Azariah beside him. Daniel had only a second to throw his mother a kiss before the guards herded them up the street like so many farm animals.

"Where are they taking us?" Mishael gasped as he stumbled amid the stampede of captives.

"To Babylon," Hananiah said, his face drawn. "They're known to take royalty hostages, you know."

"But how do they know—" Mishael realized the answer before he finished. Members of the royal family dressed differently so that the common people would show them respect. This custom benefited both the royal family and the populace, lending to an orderly society. But now it worked against the nobility, marking them as though a sign hung around their necks. Making hostages of the royal family, an ancient custom, tended to guarantee that a conquered nation would pay its taxes on time to assure the safety of captured loved ones.

Slowly the guards assembled everyone for the long march to Babylon. The soldiers forced them to discard their sandals and head coverings, and then fastened chains or ropes to wrists or ankles, forming them into long lines.

Some resisted, and found themselves shackled with both hands behind the back, elbows bound tightly together, an extremely uncomfortable position. Those who cooperated were merely tied by one wrist, leaving them comparatively free.

The lines began to move, five and six abreast, out the East Gate, down the hill, and across the Kidron Valley.

Veering left, they skirted the northwestern flank of the Mount of Olives. After passing along the shores of the Sea of Galilee, the column took the trade route to Damascus, a garden spot nestled beside the Abana River. Here Babylonian guards and captives both found rest from the rigors of their journey.

After the brief reprieve, the 10,000 forlorn prisoners trudged northward through Helbon, Zedad, Hamath, and on to Carchemish on the Euphrates River—almost 400 miles in less than a month. During the march their feet had at first blistered, then become torn and bloodied. But now most had healed and callused over. Some captives had fallen exhausted by the way. Merciless guards cut them from the line and left them to die. A few found rescue from friendly travelers, but most expired alone.

"Do not fear," Daniel encouraged his friends. "Isaiah told us that, remember? 'Do not fear, for I am with you; do not be dismayed, for I am your God. I will strengthen you and help you; I will uphold you with my righteous right hand.'"[1]

"Keep it to yourself," scoffed another who shuffled nearby. "Where is God now? He certainly didn't save us from this sorry mess. And what about Nebuchadnezzar's theft of the sacred vessels? God can't even protect His house, let alone His people!"

"It does look bad," the young prince replied. "The prophets warned us this would be sure to happen if we didn't repent and return to God. But if you'll trust in God, He'll give you peace—even if you're chained behind a Babylonian chariot."

"I'd like to believe that," the young man moaned. "I wanted to become a wealthy merchant and travel to exotic places, as my father did. But now I'll likely end up in some dungeon or become slave to a pagan lord."

"Oh, but you are traveling," Daniel chided. "And you

are seeing exotic places. If you'd trust God, your other dreams might come true as well."

"You really think so?"

"I don't know for sure. I'm no prophet. But God said: 'Those who honor me I will honor.'² And Isaiah promised: 'You will keep in perfect peace him whose mind is steadfast, because he trusts in you.'³ So if you trust Yahweh, no matter what happens you'll have peace in your heart. Isn't that worth something?"

"It sounds good," the other man replied soberly.

The captives enjoyed passing through the Carchemish ford. The cool water soothed aching muscles and brought relief from the heat.

"Let them enjoy themselves," one of the officers announced. "Nebuchadnezzar wants them to arrive in good health, and we still have a long way to go."

❀❀

"We've walked for two months," Mishael complained as he wiped his sweaty forehead. "How much longer till we get to Babylon?"

"Any day now," Hananiah replied. "The guards are talking a lot about home these days. It shouldn't be far."

For several days they had traveled well-used roads through palm groves, fields, and tiny villages, stopping frequently for rest. The highways swarmed with traffic—tradesmen, mounted messengers, carts, chariots, and farmers. Some hissed at the exiles and shouted obscenities, but most showed only mild curiosity.

When the captives sighted Babylon, they marveled at its size. Jerusalem covered no more than 20 acres, but Babylon measured more than a mile square. A double-wall system with water moats, numerous towers, and massive gates surrounded the city.

39

Gate of the Gods

Throngs of people lined the Processional Way to see the conquering army and their weary prisoners.

Approaching the Ishtar Gate, the captives passed through a narrow canyon of defensive walls several hundred feet long. The walls seemed to dance with hundreds of glazed brick animals. Each figure had its own distinctive color: yellow bulls had blue hair with green hoofs and horns; white lions had yellow manes; yellow lions had red manes; dragonlike creatures had yellow heads and tails, scaled bodies, and the feet of eagles or cats. The entire menagerie paraded across a blue background.

Inside the gate the captives passed the temple of Ninmah, mother of the gods, with its towers and vertical grooves. They could see other temples down Processional Way, but sightseeing wasn't on the day's agenda. Instead they shuffled into the palace courtyard just inside the Ishtar Gate. The large courtyard could not contain all the captives at once, so many had to stand in the street while guards distributed them to various prison blocks for detainment.

"What a dismal place," Hananiah commented as they descended the baked brick steps into a dungeon under the main palace.

"At least it's out of the hot sun," Azariah sighed.

A guard interrupted them. He spoke little Hebrew, and slaughtered the words he used. "Peaces to yous, boys," he said with glee. "Wees got really happys to see yous. Listen now. Yous trouble to us? Wees skin yous alive. Understand? Yous no trouble? Living long time."

Jailers hustled the captives down darkened hallways and shoved them into small cubicles. A guard pushed Daniel so hard that he lost his footing and sprawled onto a pile of moldy straw in the far corner. A rat scurried for safety as Daniel thrashed around to regain his footing.

Daniel strained to see in the dim light of the cell as his

three companions stumbled into the room. The door clanked shut behind them. The rough walls consisted of fired brick fitted together so closely that digging through them seemed out of the question. The small hole near the ceiling admitted little air and even less light. He staunched a wave of nausea caused by the stench of sweat, urine, and sewage that permeated the room. But the rustle of rats gave him the shivers, for he knew he'd have to sleep on their level.

The four young men sat on their putrid straw in silence. The curses of other captives filled the air, and the sound of someone vomiting only stirred their stomachs more.

"We'll die here!" Mishael exclaimed. "We can't survive a week in this place."

Hananiah pressed a finger to Mishael's lips. "Sh-h-h." Tears trickled down his own cheeks. "But for the providence of God, we'll all perish. But I believe—" He wiped his tears with his sleeve. "I believe that God will sustain us."

"My thoughts exactly," Daniel added. "'Do not fear, for I am with you,'" he began, and the others joined him. "'Do not be dismayed, for I am your God. I will strengthen you and help you; I will uphold you with my righteous right hand.'"[4]

The cell seemed to lighten, the rats grew quiet, and their stomachs began to settle.

---

[1] Isaiah 41:10.
[2] 1 Samuel 2:30.
[3] Isaiah 26:3.
[4] Isaiah 41:10.

Conflict

Trumpets sang out in the royal salute for the return of King Nebuchadnezzar from the wars. City walls bristled with both excited soldiers and civilians who marveled at the size of the approaching army. Had it been an enemy, they would have panicked. Instead, they swelled with pride.

The sheer size of the army radiated power. Brilliant-colored banners flickered above triumphant squadrons, carried aloft on spears. But the eyes of spectators focused on the ornate vehicle moving near the center of the seething horde. Pulled by eight white stallions and dwarfing all others, the portable throne bore the king of Babylon. The royal vehicle had a fringed canopy, and displayed carvings of cult symbols and previous battles. Nebuchadnezzar, in royal battle dress, rode on this miniature castle on wheels, flanked by dozens of servants.

Thousands cheered the oncoming host and searched for family members who had accompanied them. The troops responded by chanting battle slogans: "Nebuchadnezzar the magnificent conquers all!" "Babylon, the pride of the nations, will reign supreme!" "May Lord Marduk subdue all his enemies!" The tumult hurt everyone's ears, but excitement overshadowed pain, and no one wanted to stop. Lord Nebuchadnezzar had returned to his people. Babylon the Great had proven victorious once again!

Nebuchadnezzar received divine sanction from the hands of Marduk anew at the New Year's festival. Again the high priest's slap brought tears to his eyes, and again the prelate pronounced Marduk's blessing for the coming year.

The great king presented the priests many trophies that he'd collected during his campaign, among them gold, silver, and brass utensils from the Temple of Yahweh in Jerusalem. These they would display in a museum known as the "Treasure House of Esagila."

Nebuchadnezzar retired to his palace—a vast complex of buildings bordered by the Processional Way, the Euphrates River, and the Libilhegalla Canal. At the palace entrance huge basalt lions guarded the Beltis Gate, which opened into the eastern court. This enclosure, the first of five courts that led to the throne room, buzzed with ceaseless activity. Surrounding the courtyards stood army stations, government offices, private apartments, and the royal harem.

In the main courtyard, a large group of nobles gathered around him, Nebuchadnezzar brought out his most valuable prizes—articles of gold and silver, jewels, wood and ivory carvings, and other works of art captured during raids in Syria and Palestine. These he put on display in his own museum.

Because he had been away for months, many important matters awaited his attention—squabbles between wealthy nobles, legal cases too difficult for lower judges, tax disputes, and criminal executions. Nebuchadnezzar found himself submerged in affairs of state for weeks, and the work exhausted him.

"This business is important," he remarked to his chamberlain one day during a rest between appointments. "But it's so much more tiring than field campaigns."

"That it is, my lord."

"I can see why many kings spend most of their time waging war." Nebuchadnezzar descended the steps of his throne and wandered about the courtyard, examining his latest trophies. "Combat is so much more exciting than these dreary days at court."

"True," his chamberlain agreed. "But war creates pain and suffering. Your work here has brought peace to many troubled hearts."

"You think so?" The king seemed surprised.

"Of course, my lord. To whom can these people turn for settlement of their problems but to you, O king? And once you've reached a decision, the matter is settled. Then the people can use their time and energies in more constructive ways."

"You speak wisdom," the young monarch mused. "I'd never thought of it that way."

"If it please the king." The chamberlain bowed.

"Continue."

"War is sometimes necessary to defend homeland, or punish offending nations—and it brings treasure into the king's coffers. But think how much greater blessing a king could be to his people if he found peaceful ways to settle international disputes, and spent his time instead building up his own nation, encouraging his people, and strengthening their hands."

"You've given me a lot to think about," the king replied as he signaled for a servant to usher in the next petitioner.

⁂

"Ashpenaz." Nebuchadnezzar summoned the master of the eunuchs into his presence.

The man bowed at the waist, moved forward until he stood before the throne, and then straightened. "May the king live forever."

"Examine the captives in our dungeons," the king began, "and select those of royal blood who have no physical imperfections about them—handsome, wise, and already acquainted with science and politics. Bring me the very best. I want to train them to work for me."

"Yes, my lord." The palace official left the courtyard and descended into the dungeons. He knew them well, for he had often used prisoners to fill bureaucratic positions in Babylon.

Accompanied by guards and torchbearers, Ashpenaz passed from cell to putrid cell, examining the men and choosing the few who met the king's standards. He had never liked the stench of this place, but he ignored it and concentrated on his job.

He had worked for more than an hour when he came to a cell in which the floors had been swept. The four men inside, though dressed in filthy rags like the others, stood at attention, clothes arranged as neatly as possible. *Odd behavior in a dungeon,* he thought.

"What's your name?" Ashpenaz spoke in flawless Hebrew, one of his many languages.

"Daniel, my lord." He smiled and bowed politely. "I'm of the royal house of Judah."

Ashpenaz could hardly control his astonishment. This young man had been dragged a thousand miles from home and locked up like an animal, yet he maintained his dignity.

"And you?" He pointed to the others.

"Hananiah."

"Mishael."

"Azariah."

"They also belong to Judah's royal family," Daniel added.

The court official gazed at the quartet for a moment and then spoke to the prison guard in Aramaic. "Clean them up, clothe them, and have them in the eastern courtyard first thing in the morning."

"By your command, my lord."

The master of the eunuchs continued his tour, but he couldn't forget those four dignified hostages. "I've never seen anything like that before," he mused aloud as he left the prison. "Remarkable men. They should prove valuable in the king's service."

❧❧

The sun bathed the Processional Way as several dozen prisoners assembled in the eastern palace courtyard. They had washed, dressed in clean new clothes, and now, for the first time in weeks, felt a sense of hope.

"What a gorgeous place!" Azariah exclaimed as his eyes adjusted to the light. "Look at all those animals pictured on the walls. With artists like that, why would they ever covet Judah's humble finery?"

"It is beautiful," Hananiah said. "But I daresay they didn't come to Judah for our art. They came for gold."

"Shhh!" Daniel cautioned as a trumpet sounded. "I think the king is coming."

Nebuchadnezzar strode into the courtyard surrounded by guards and palace officials. He didn't go directly to the throne, but strolled before the captives, studying them with interest, stopping now and then for a closer look at one person or another.

As he came opposite Daniel and his friends, he paused. Daniel, standing in the third row, thought at first that the king was examining a man in the front. But no, the royal eyes gazed at Daniel. The captive felt self-conscious, wanting to glance away. And yet he couldn't take his eyes off the king. *Strange,* he thought, *Nebuchadnezzar doesn't appear any older than I do.* His spine began to tingle at something in the king's expression. Somehow the young Jew felt that the two must have—or would have—a great deal in common.

The moment seemed to last forever as absolute monarch

46

and conquered hostage locked gaze. But then it passed, and the king continued surveying the others.

After Nebuchadnezzar had seated himself, he turned to Ashpenaz, who stood to one side of the captives. "You have chosen well. I accept them all."

Then he explained his plan to the captives. "I've selected you because you have abilities that could benefit my kingdom." He paused and held a whispered conversation with his chamberlain.

"I have," he continued after a moment, "chosen you to serve in positions of trust. Today I am adopting you as members of the royal family, and you will be treated as princes. You will receive new names to show the honor that I have bestowed, and will live in the palace, your food and wine coming from my table."

The captives' faces reflected surprise at their good fortune as a low murmur spread through their ranks. Ashpenaz frowned and held up his hand for silence.

"You will need training, of course," the king resumed, "so Rabsaris Ashpenaz will enroll you in the palace academy, where you'll receive the same education required of the royal family.

"After three years I will examine you myself. Those who achieve good marks will receive honor and high offices. I'm counting on you to do your best. May Lord Marduk give you success."

꘡꘡

"Did you hear what the king said about food?" Mishael asked as the four settled into their new quarters. The room, though small, bore the same pagan motifs they had seen throughout the palace.

"Yes," Hananiah said. "They plan to serve us the food prepared for the king—a great honor, I'm sure."

"But that means—" Mishael glanced out the door to

make sure that no guards could overhear. "That means they'll serve us swine's flesh. The Scriptures say that we're not supposed to eat that."

"They'll also feed us meats that have been offered to idols," Azariah added. "If we eat those, we'll be denying Yahweh and worshipping the gods of Babylon."

"And they'll serve us all the wine that we could ever want," Hananiah reminded them. "But it seems to me that Moses' story about Nadab and Abihu's death reveals how God feels when people drink things that take away their ability to reason."

The four sat in silence for several minutes. They no longer rotted in a dank dungeon, but their situation had become even more critical. Though showered with worldly advantages, they now stood in danger of losing their relationship with God.

Daniel smiled at his cousins' dilemma. "Remember how we agreed to be true to God no matter what happened?"

"Yes," they chorused.

"Well, now we've come to a test of our resolve. We can accept the king's favors and enjoy great honor in Babylon. Or we can stand for the right and perhaps lose everything— maybe even our lives. Especially since eating from the king's table is also a sign of political loyalty. To spurn some of his food will be perceived as a rejection of his sovereignty."

"Pretty big decision," Hananiah sighed.

"Yes, it is," Daniel agreed. "And one we dare not make without consulting Yahweh."

The four young men knelt facing west, toward Jerusalem. Solomon, in his Temple dedication prayer, had asked God to respond to all prayers directed toward the Temple, and they needed Him to hear them now, more than ever.

"O Lord God," Daniel prayed, "we did not come to Babylon because of our own choice. They brought us here as captives because of our sins, and the sins of our fathers. Although we have been separated from our families and from daily worship in the Temple, we know that our lives are within Your hands. Thus we believe that You will help and sustain us. Grant us wisdom to know what we should do, and then give us courage to do it."

As they rose, Daniel began to quote a psalm that Jeremiah had taught them, and the others joined him:

> "Your commands make me wiser than my enemies,
>   for they are ever with me.
> I have more insight than all my teachers,
>   for I meditate on your statutes.
> I have more understanding than the elders,
>   for I obey your precepts.
> I have kept my feet from every evil path
>   so that I might obey your word."[1]

"I believe we'll gain a victory for Yahweh," Daniel continued, "only if we do the right thing—because it is right. We'll not succeed in the palace school because of chance or accident or destiny, but only through faithfulness to God and earnest effort on our part. I don't think we have any other choice than to obey Yahweh, whatever the cost. I will not eat the king's meats, nor will I drink the wine from his table."

"I agree," Hananiah said. "If we eat the king's rich food we'll not be able to think clearly, and we'll surely fall into sin."

"It's not going to be easy," Mishael reminded. "But I'm with you."

"Me too," Azariah added.

"Then it's settled." Daniel smiled at his friends. "Now let's see if we can find a way to avoid trouble for ourselves—and our teachers."

❦❦

Ashpenaz thanked his lucky stars that he had found such good students for the palace school. He had grown up in the royal family of Persia, and, though taken hostage by Nabopolassar, had received a high office in the Babylonian government. Now he smiled at the thought of helping other royal captives in Babylon.

Out of the hundreds he had interviewed, none had been so remarkable as Daniel and his three friends. Most captives were still bitter about their situation, and many, when given positions of trust, became arrogant. But not Daniel. He had a modesty and meekness that Ashpenaz had never seen before. The royal official felt a growing fondness for the four young Judahites.

Late on the first day Ashpenaz looked up from his work in the dining hall to see Daniel and his friends approaching.

"Daniel!" The Persian's joy could not be contained. "I'm so happy you were chosen for the rotal training program."

Bowing politely, Daniel smiled. "We are pleased as well, my lord. But we have a matter we need to discuss with you."

"Of course."

Briefly Daniel related their beliefs and the crisis they faced. "Would you be so kind as to serve us cereals and vegetables and dates and other fruits instead of the king's rich food and wine? You have plenty of these kinds of foods in the palace storerooms."

The official's smile faded. He had never heard of anyone refusing to eat food prepared for a king and realized as well the political implications of such an act. "I–I don't know," he stammered. For an instant he felt confused. "I'm not sure I understand, Daniel. The king has granted all his subjects the right to worship as they please. But if I don't feed you well, you'll become ill, and the king will be angry with me. I might lose my job—perhaps even my head."

The master of the eunuchs gazed at the four healthy men

who stood before him. How could they survive on such a bland diet? Everyone knew that rich food promoted good physical health and greater mental activity. Besides, he had no authority to change the king's order, and Nebuchadnezzar would probably never agree to it.

"No, Daniel," he answered kindly but firmly. "I can't alter the king's command. You'll just have to serve your god as best you can—while you eat what the king has provided."

Daniel saw that the official would not waver, so he bowed politely, thanked the man, and retreated with his friends.

"What will we do?" Mishael agonized.

"Don't despair," Daniel replied. "We haven't come to the end of our hope yet."

The four strolled to their assigned table and seated themselves in the prescribed order. Wine had already been poured and the cups arranged neatly on the table.

Other students began to arrive, and soon the room vibrated with the chatter of young men. The effect of the wine only loosened their wagging tongues all the more.

"Pardon me, sir." Daniel spoke to an instructor who passed their table. "You're the melzar,[2] aren't you?"

"Why, yes. And you must be Daniel."

"That's right." Choosing his words carefully, Daniel explained their predicament to this servant who would have charge of their training. "Sir, this is important to us. We'd like to propose an experiment. Grant our request for 10 days. By then you'll know whether our diet will bring us good or evil."

The melzar liked Daniel's earnestness. *What a fine student,* he thought. "Why not?" he said aloud. "Might be interesting. Mind you, I don't think you'll do well on such a bland diet, but I doubt that 10 days will do you any real harm."

"Thank you, sir," the young men chorused.

"Now, my lord," Daniel said as he set the cups of wine

on a tray and handed it to the melzar, "if you'd be so kind as to get us some water."

✻✻

"You must be crazy!" sneered a Jewish youth to Daniel after supper. "I heard what you told that heathen about vegetables and water. I'm surprised he didn't have you impaled!" The young man spat out the words as other students gathered around, echoing his objections.

"You'll cause trouble for all of us if you keep this up," shouted another. "And you'll lose your position—maybe your life—if you treat the Babylonians like this."

Daniel calmly faced his angry fellows. "Isn't the favor of God worth more than the honors of Babylon? I'd rather die than disobey my Creator."

"But Daniel," another protested, "if you'd just bend a little—if you'd forget the useless requirements of our religion—in the end you'd be able to accomplish great good."

"It may seem that way," Daniel said softly, "but God can never bless us if we disobey Him—even in little things. If I obey one of God's laws because it's convenient and ignore another because it would require sacrifice, then I'm turning my back on God and becoming a law unto myself.

"There's another important point to think about," he continued. "God gave us our bodies so that we could serve Him. If we don't take care of them, we'll not be able to think clearly enough to tell the difference between good and evil. Anything that harms our health makes it that much easier for us to fall into sin."

"That makes sense," someone observed after a moment's consideration.

"What is this?" someone demanded. "Are you joining them?"

The young man backed off, but no longer joined the

others in challenging Daniel's behavior. Through the years to come he and several others would learn to know and worship God through the witness of Daniel and his friends.

※※

Ashpenaz stood before Nebuchadnezzar, ready to report on the status of his students. He congratulated himself on their progress and felt sure they would be ready for graduation in three years. But Nebuchadnezzar unnerved the prince with his first question.

"What's this I hear about students refusing to eat my food?" Nebuchadnezzar seemed irritated.

"Daniel, my lord?"

"Yes, Ashpenaz. And his three companions. What's going on?"

The official's face turned pale. Though he had refused Daniel's request, he had chosen to ignore the melzar's acceptance of it.

"This Daniel is a rare person," Ashpenaz began, feeling that his knees would buckle at any moment. "He has genuine meekness, does his work well, refuses to be false in anything—a noble young man. Although he keeps peace with everyone, my lord, he stands like a lofty cedar whenever his religion is threatened. I do believe he'd rather die than disobey his God."

"Yes, yes, Ashpenaz," the king interrupted. "I've noticed that too. But what about the experiment? How did it go?"

The official marveled at the king's knowledge of what went on in his palace. "Well, my lord, at the end of the 10-day trial we found the results opposite from what we'd expected. Daniel and his friends were superior to the other captives in personal appearance and in physical strength. They seemed to have more mental vigor as well."

"Amazing!" Nebuchadnezzar breathed. "I would never

have thought that a change of food could make so much difference."

"It seems to have done so in this case, my lord."

The king smiled. "Allowing them to carry on such an experiment without my permission was risky for you, Ashpenaz."

"I-I know, my lord." The official dropped his head, fearing royal disapproval.

"Well, I don't see any reason to change their diet now. Let them continue eating their vegetables. We'll see what happens. But from now on, consult me before you allow any more experiments."

----

[1] Psalm 119:98-101.

[2] "Warden," "guardian."

Chapter 4

"Rising Star"

"The Aramaic language hasn't really been all that diffi-cult," Azariah said at lunch one day. "It's similar to Hebrew because our ancestors came from this area." He took a hand-ful of dates from the bowl on the table.

"It's not the language of the common people of Babylon, either," Mishael observed. "The Chaldean rulers from south-ern Mesopotamia have evidently forced it on the empire as the language of international diplomacy."

"Yes," Azariah returned. "And everyone who lives here seems to speak at least two languages—some even more."

"I remember hearing merchants in the Jerusalem bazaar speak this tongue," Hananiah said. "I thought it strange then. But it's not so hard to understand now."

"No, it's not," Mishael agreed. "The language isn't diffi-cult, but their method of writing has me in a bind. These cuneiform letters look like so many bird scratches, and there's no end of them. They have hundreds of different characters, some with only small differences in meaning."

"And yet you're doing better than most other students," Hananiah reminded him. "In fact, your progress is remark-able considering that you've studied it less than a year."

"We're all doing well." Daniel smiled as he took his seat and helped himself to some dried fruit.

"That's true, isn't it," Mishael remarked. "Why are we doing so much better than the others?"

"God has helped us learn more quickly than the other

students," Daniel replied. "Remember His promise through Samuel? 'Those who honor me I will honor.'* We have obeyed His word and trusted Him to care for us, and He has given us good health and quick minds."

☆☆

At a ceremony early in their training, each student received a new name to show that he belonged to Babylon's royal family. The names had been chosen in the hope that the captive bearing it would assimilate to the culture and religion of their new home.

Daniel received the name Belteshazzar, which meant "may [Bel, the god Marduk] protect his life." Hananiah became Shadrach, "command of Aku [a Mesopotamian lunar deity]." Mishael was now called Meshach ("who is that which Aku is"), and Azariah was renamed Abednego—"a servant of [Nebuchadnezzar's personal god] Nabu."

Though Babylonian officials always used the new names, Daniel and his friends continued calling each other by their Hebrew ones.

☆☆

"Let's review this again," Mishael requested as he squinted at an astronomical chart drawn on a baked clay tablet. Azariah, Hananiah, and Daniel bent over the table and concentrated on their cousin's review.

"If I'm right, the moon and sun pass through the star groupings known as the zodiac. The sun makes a complete circuit once each year, while the moon goes around every month."

"That's right," Daniel said. "And the planets Mercury, Venus, Mars, Jupiter, and Saturn ride within the same star path, each having its own period."

"But how can the astrologers know when an eclipse will

happen," Azariah inquired, "or when the planets will be closest to each other?"

"They've kept records for centuries measuring the time it takes for each heavenly body to make its round, as well as the path it follows," Daniel explained. "From this information they can calculate the exact positions of the sun, moon, and planets for any night in any year."

Hananiah let out a low whistle. "Fantastic!"

"Yes, it is," Daniel agreed. "It's just too bad that they think these heavenly bodies are gods."

"And they believe that these so-called gods actually guide them in their daily activities," Azariah commented. "I guess that's why the astrologers have such power over the king. He believes they have a direct channel of communication with the gods."

"Well, we know better." Mishael smiled. "It would be so easy to accept pagan teachings if we didn't already know that Yahweh created all these things."

The three-year course of study slipped by, and the final examination drew near. Tension mounted throughout the palace school, for each student knew that his entire future depended upon his performance—whether good or bad.

"Will the princes be ready for the examination?" Nebuchadnezzar asked one day.

"Yes, my lord," Ashpenaz replied. "They have made excellent progress, and I'm sure that my lord the king will be gratified with the results."

"How about those vegetable eaters from Judah? Have they kept up with the others?"

"Yes, my lord. In fact, they've surpassed them in every way." Ashpenaz smiled as he remembered his own doubts. "My lord will be pleased, for those young men are the king's finest."

"We'll see." Nebuchadnezzar appeared unimpressed. But his curiosity grappled with the concept of the strange diet and its apparent success.

At last the final day arrived. The students stood at attention while Nebuchadnezzar gave the examination. Each contestant answered questions that His Majesty had devised to test their ability to make wise decisions instantly. He also watched to see how they worked under pressure—and he knew of no greater stress than for a young captive to stand before the king, knowing that his entire future hung on the answers to a few questions.

"How many months in the year?" Nebuchadnezzar asked the first student.

"Twelve months, my lord," the young man answered, "and each month contains 30 days."

"H'mmm," the king mumbled. "That would account for 360 days. So what are we supposed to do with the other five?"

"We add an extra month at regular intervals, my lord."

"How often do we add this extra month?"

"I-I'm not sure, my lord." The student scratched his head. "I guess we'd have to consult the charts."

"Explain the use of the sundial," the king questioned another.

"The sunlight falls on the dial's arm and casts a shadow across a graduated circle drawn around the arm." The student visibly swallowed hard. "We can tell the time of day by reading the numbers on the dial."

"How do you know which direction to point the sundial?"

"I don't know, my lord." The young man looked down at his sandals. "I've always consulted dials that had already been put in place."

One by one the students stood before the king. Some answered well, but others seemed ignorant of even basic knowledge. A number still had difficulty speaking the Aramaic language, and failed even to understand the gist of Nebuchadnezzar's questions.

"How do we count the years of a king's reign?"

The student stood erect, with no outward sign of stress,

and returned the king's gaze with steady eyes. "The first year of the king's reign is known as his 'accession year.'" Daniel's voice didn't quaver, and his explanation appeared flawless. "On the first New Year's Day after the king has come to the throne, he begins his first year of reign."

"Does it make any difference how long that accession year is?"

"No. It can be any length, from one day to 11 months and 29 days."

"What year is this in my reign?"

"This is your second year of reign."

"But I've been on the throne for three years, young man." The king spoke harshly, testing Daniel's nerve.

"That's true, my lord. However, the first was your accession year, so this is actually your second year of reign."

"Where do our merchants get emeralds?"

"From India, my lord."

"Pearls?"

"From the coast of the Red Sea."

"Why do we base our numbering system on 60s instead of 10s, as the other nations do?"

"The base 60 system has many advantages." Daniel's voice remained even and well modulated, his muscles relaxed. "For one thing, it is divisible by 12 factors instead of only nine—as in the case of base 10 systems—and it seems ideal for measuring time and angles, my lord."

The questions continued. Time swept by, and the sun descended toward the western horizon. Students and teachers, though uncomfortable from standing in the hot sun, became engrossed by the knowledge and poise of the exile from Judah.

Nebuchadnezzar gazed into the bright eyes of the young captive prince before him. He listened enthralled at Daniel's explanations. The answers never erred and often presented material clearly logical in concept, but unknown to the king.

The other three Hebrews had also impressed the king, but Daniel excelled them all. The king could find nothing that Daniel didn't know or couldn't reason out in a few words. And yet he remained so calm, so self-possessed.

Most of those who passed Nebuchadnezzar's examination, despite their deficiencies, received jobs at various levels of the Babylonian bureaucracy. But Daniel had the distinction of being the only one chosen as a member of the king's inner circle. And Daniel's friends—Shadrach, Meshach, and Abednego—also found themselves filling positions of great responsibility in the empire.

"In my court," the king announced, "I've gathered men of the highest talent from all lands. And yet, today, four young men from the little kingdom of Judah have outstripped them."

"I agree, my lord," Ashpenaz replied. "They stand without a peer."

"Did you see them?" the king asked as if he hadn't heard. "They stood so straight and tall—their graceful walk, their smooth skin, their untainted breath! Could diet have that much effect?"

"It would seem so, my lord." Ashpenaz, too, seemed lost in thought.

For several moments neither spoke as each silently reviewed the examination of the last four candidates. Nebuchadnezzar had liked Daniel from the day he saw him standing in the courtyard with the other captives. Now he knew why. Something about this exile from Judah appealed to the young king.

"The Spirit of his God must be in him." Nebuchadnezzar broke the long silence. "A brilliant star has risen this day, Lord Ashpenaz. A star that will light all Babylon's future."

---

* 1 Samuel 2:30.

Chapter 5

Dream of Destiny

"Is there anything else my lord desires?" the king's valet asked as he dressed his master for the night.

Nebuchadnezzar showed no sign that he had heard the question, so the servant continued his routine.

Babylonian kings were never alone. Whether day or night, servants, guards, court officials, wives, or children surrounded them—most quietly performing their duties, but some causing considerable distraction. Even when the king slept, servants and guards waited outside doors and windows, protecting the monarch and his family, ready to fetch anything the royal whim might desire.

Tonight Nebuchadnezzar seemed lost in thought as the servant removed his sandals and set them on a shelf near his bed. The valet washed his master's feet in cool water, dried them with a soft linen towel, and poured the used water down the toilet hole in an adjoining cubicle. The waste disappeared into a pipe that passed under the palace and into the Euphrates River.

The servant dressed the king in his nightshirt, pulled back his bedcovers, and, when Nebuchadnezzar had reclined, tucked him in—much as a mother would her little child. Then, bowing, he retired to his own room adjoining the royal bedchamber, ready at any moment to answer the king's bidding.

The Babylonian monarch lay awake, thinking. Earlier that evening he had visited his harem, consoling his favorite wife, the princess Amuhia. But he had already forgotten those joys. His tedious day at court—planning and making decisions—seemed far away. Staring into the semidarkness, his mind even tuned out the distant croak of frogs and the chirping of crickets.

I wonder what lies ahead, he mused. *My father built this empire, and I've enlarged it. No other kingdom on earth can equal mine. No empire in history has ever come close! I wonder. Will my kingdom last 100 years?. . . Perhaps 1,000? Will it . . . last . . . forever?*

❀❀

Nebuchadnezzar jolted from sleep, terror flooding him. Had it been a dream? No, a nightmare! So awesome, so grand—so horrible! Yet, what had it been about? Unable to remember any of the details, he didn't know.

This was serious, for Babylonians believed that the gods spoke to humanity through dreams. And since Nebuchadnezzar was king, he especially could expect to receive such dream messages.

Which of the gods tried to reach me last night? he wondered. *And what did he say?* Though he tried, he couldn't even recall the general subject. "This is terrible!" he moaned. "Here I receive what must be an important dream, but I can't recall any of it."

Throwing off his covers, he bounded out of bed. "Guard," he cried, "send for my counselors—*hurry!* Where is my servant?" The sleepy valet scurried into the room. "There he is." Nebuchadnezzar jabbered in a frenzy. "Bring my clothes! My advisors will be here any minute."

No time for the usual bath, massage, manicure, and hairstyling. The valet draped his master with clothes as he rushed out the door, guards double-timing it to keep up.

As Nebuchadnezzar reached the court, several counselors had already arrived, though some still adjusted clothing or combed hair and beards. All seemed drowsy, for they too had been jerked from slumber, with no opportunity to eat or prepare for the day.

Next to the king himself, these unkempt men held the most important jobs in the kingdom. They revealed to the monarch what the gods wanted him to do. By using their religious crafts, they said, they could read the future, reveal secrets, and give advice that would ensure the ruler's success in any venture. Bowing, they approached the king with their faces toward the ground.

Nebuchadnezzar came right to the point. "I have had a dream that troubles me, and I want to know what it was."[1]

The royal counselors rubbed their sleepy eyes and looked at each other in surprise. Had they heard right?

"O king, live forever!" their leader droned in a monotone voice. "Tell your servants the dream, and we will interpret it."

The king's eyes narrowed as he studied those before him. He had always trusted them. But now, when in desperate need, he somehow felt they had nothing of value to give.

A web of dread tightened in the pit of his stomach. Messages from gods often related to a particular moment and, if not obeyed within the allotted time, would cause the loss of the promised blessing—or, worse yet, the receipt of the threatened curse. And the men he trusted to guide him now balked at what he thought a reasonable request—to reveal his dream and tell him what it meant.

Had they been deceiving him all this time? He decided to find out. Perhaps a little threat would reveal their honesty!

"This is what I have firmly decided." Nebuchadnezzar's voice had a razor-sharp edge. "If you do not tell me what my dream was and interpret it, I will have you cut into pieces and your houses turned into piles of rubble. But if you tell me the dream and explain it, you will receive from me gifts and rewards and great honor. So tell me the dream and interpret it for me."

The counselors' foggy brains snapped to attention. "Let

the king tell his servants the dream, and we will interpret it," they repeated.

Aha! thought the king. *They have been cheating! And now they're trying to worm their way out of it. I'll increase the threat a little further. Then I'll know for sure.*

"I am certain that you are trying to gain time, because you realize that this is what I have firmly decided: If you do not tell me the dream, there is just one penalty for you. So then, tell me the dream, and I will know that you can interpret it for me."

The terrified counselors found themselves caught between impossibility and annihilation. "There is not a man on earth who can do what the king asks!" they exclaimed, fear etching their guilty faces. "No king, however great and mighty, has ever asked such a thing. No one can reveal it to the king except the gods, and they do not live among men."

Impostors! Nebuchadnezzar thought. *They've always claimed they could reveal divine secrets, but now when I need them, I find they're frauds.* His heart pounded, and blood rushed into his face as surprise transformed into rage.

"Away with them!" he screamed. "Destroy all the wise men of Babylon. They're all a bunch of liars and cheats!"

The counselors shrank back, their faces pale, terror tying tight knots in their intestines. Before they could run, the king's guards surrounded them and herded them into another courtyard to be held prisoner until armed men could round up the other wise men—with all their wives and children.

Nebuchadnezzar sank onto his throne in agony, his body limp, his stomach a blazing inferno. "What have I done?" he gasped. His mind reeled at the swift events of the past few minutes. Though only 20 years old, he had a strong sense of justice and abhorred the misuse of power. But now in the heat of passion he had condemned to death the innocent wives and children of his conniving counselors.

"Chamberlain!" He beckoned the official who had slipped into the courtyard. "Bring me wine and food. I haven't eaten yet."

The man bowed and turned to leave.

"Never mind the food," the king called after him. "Just the wine—hurry."

The chamberlain poured the wine into a golden goblet, tasted it for poison, and then served it to the monarch.

"I really made a mess of that one," the young monarch confessed to the only man with whom he felt any degree of intimacy. "I wish I could take it all back . . . without losing face."

"Yes, my lord," mused the chamberlain. "But your command was quite final. If you rescind it, you'll weaken your authority."

※※

Arioch, the chief executioner, had enjoyed a somewhat relaxed agenda during the past two years, for Nebuchadnezzar had been humane compared with many rulers. He had dispatched a few criminals and some onerous prisoners taken in the wars, but otherwise few had lost their heads.

Now he had a big job. Although he had become accustomed to brutality and often took pride in his efficiency, his present assignment seemed distasteful. He saw nothing unusual about executing entire families, for in his culture families often suffered the fate of the specific offender among them, as unfair as that might sometimes appear—even to the chief executioner. But the entire royal cabinet? Now, that did appear a bit out of the ordinary.

Never mind, he thought. *The king decrees—I obey. Who knows? Their families may be just as guilty.* So while his guards held the chief counselors captive, he and his men swept the city for other condemned officials and all their families.

He worked down a list given him by a palace scribe. At

each house he knocked gently on the door, bowed, and politely explained the king's order, then lined up all family members in the street to watch in anguish as his men wrecked their house. Then his guards led the condemned family to the courtyard-turned-prison to await their execution.

The sun had climbed high into the sky when Arioch called at his last house—that of a recently elevated counselor.

"Why did the king issue such a harsh decree?" Belteshazzar, the king's youngest counselor, asked when he learned the man's mission. "You have a difficult task." Daniel put his hand on the court official's shoulder. "But there may be a way we can spare you this terrible task."

Arioch didn't understand at first. But Daniel's compassion caused him to recognize even further the carnage he and his men would inflict before the day's end—the human suffering, the pain, the death. Suddenly he felt intensely alone. He gazed into the eyes of the young man he had just summoned to death and realized that Daniel had not spoken of saving himself. No, he had said, "Perhaps we can spare you." The man had shown concern for his own executioner!

"Take me to the king." Daniel's gentle command overcame all the lethargy that had overwhelmed Arioch during the day's gruesome activities. Without thinking, he motioned for the young man to follow. Leaving his men in the street, he led the way to the palace.

When Daniel confronted Nebuchadnezzar, the king seemed relieved to find a way out. He had always been impressed with Belteshazzar, so he granted him time and ordered a temporary stay of execution.

Daniel and his friends spent much time that evening in prayer. And God heard them. That night He revealed Nebuchadnezzar's dream to Daniel. When Daniel awoke, he began to sing:

"He changes times and seasons;
  he sets up kings and deposes them.
  He gives wisdom to the wise
  and knowledge to the discerning.
  He reveals deep and hidden things;
  he knows what lies in darkness,
  and light dwells with him.
  I thank and praise you, O God of my fathers:
  You have given me wisdom and power,
  you have made known to me what we asked of you,
  you have made known to us the dream of the king."[2]

"Do not execute the wise men of Babylon," Daniel called as he hurried to Arioch at the palace guardhouse. "Take me to the king, and I will interpret his dream for him."

The chief executioner smiled. "Good. Follow me."

Nebuchadnezzar's sleep had been even more fitful than the night before, and he felt irritable as he seated himself on his throne. Still worried about the dream and the fate of the condemned counselors, he had no patience for the legal cases that faced him, and yet his sense of duty drove him to dispense justice to all who required it. Justice! He scowled, guilt well-nigh crushing his soul. *How can I judge the most insignificant dispute when I condemn innocents to die?*

At that moment Arioch strode into court, Daniel close on his heels and looking as calm as a summer's eve. The chief executioner spoke as he bowed. "My lord, I have found a man among the exiles from Judah who can tell the king what his dream means."

Hope sprang anew within the king's heart. "Wonderful!" he shouted, turning to Daniel. "Belteshazzar. Are you able to tell me what I saw in my dream—and interpret it?"

Daniel instantly sensed the ruler's great distress. For once he felt satisfied to be a mere exile at peace with his God. His friendly gaze assured Nebuchadnezzar that his search had ended.

But the king bristled at Daniel's first words. "No wise man, enchanter, magician, or diviner can explain to the king the mystery he has asked about."

What? Nebuchadnezzar's anger began to surface once more, for Daniel repeated the exact words the wise men had uttered two days ago. *Has Belteshazzar sold out?*

"But—" Daniel interrupted the monarch's thoughts. "But there is a God in heaven who reveals mysteries. He has shown King Nebuchadnezzar what will happen in days to come. Your dream and the visions that passed through your mind as you lay on your bed are these."

Instantly Nebuchadnezzar recalled his mental turmoil the night before the dream and remembered his desire to know the future—to have his kingdom last forever. He leaned forward to hear this message from the God in heaven.

"As you were lying there, O king," Daniel began, "your mind turned to things to come, and the revealer of mysteries showed you what is going to happen. As for me, this mystery has been revealed to me, not because I have greater wisdom than other living men, but so that you, O king, may know the interpretation and that you may understand what went through your mind.

"You looked, O king, and there before you stood a large statue—an enormous, dazzling statue, awesome in appearance. The head of the statue consisted of pure gold, its chest and arms of silver, its belly and thighs of bronze, its legs of iron, and its feet partly of iron and partly of baked clay."

"Yes!" Nebuchadnezzar exclaimed. "That's it! That's what I saw."

"While you were watching"—Daniel politely ignored the king's interruption—"a rock was cut out, but not by human hands. It struck the statue on its feet of iron and clay and smashed them. Then the iron, the clay, the bronze, the silver, and the gold shattered to pieces at the same time and became like chaff on a threshing floor in the summer. The wind swept them away without leaving a trace. But the rock that struck the statue became a mountain and filled the earth.

"This was the dream, and now we will interpret it to the king."

Nebuchadnezzar felt elated. Belteshazzar had described his dream precisely as he had seen it two nights before, and the flood of mingled wonder and dread began to return. His mouth hung open as he waited to hear what it meant.

"The God of heaven has given you dominion and power and might and glory. In your hands He has placed humanity and the beasts of the field and the birds of the air. Wherever they live, He has made you ruler over them all. You are that head of gold."

Nebuchadnezzar had often credited his honor and success to the god Marduk. But Daniel made it clear that his real power came from the God of heaven. And the head of gold represented him—his kingdom. Pride swelled up within him. Not only had the God of heaven given him a dream, but in it he ranked number one!

But his self-esteem stumbled over itself as Daniel continued. "After you, another kingdom will rise—"

After me? My kingdom will not last forever?

"—inferior to yours. Next, a third kingdom, one of bronze, will rule over the whole earth. Finally, there will be a fourth kingdom, strong as iron—for iron breaks and smashes everything—and as iron breaks things to pieces, so it will crush all the others."

The young political hostage painted the rest of the dream for the king: the feet and toes represented a division of the iron kingdom, and afterward many would attempt to weld them together again—without success. No empire in the sense of Nebuchadnezzar's would again trample earth's people.

"In the time of those kings"—Daniel referred to the feet and toes—"the God of heaven will set up a kingdom that will never be destroyed, nor will it be left to another people. It will crush all those kingdoms and bring them to an end, but it will itself endure forever.

"The great God has shown the king what will take place in the future. The dream is true, and the interpretation is trustworthy."

Daniel's portrayal of the dream had been so accurate that Nebuchadnezzar knew he could accept the interpretation. Marveling at the knowledge of Daniel's God, he could not constrain his awe. He stumbled from his throne, fell on his face, and gave homage to Daniel as a slave would to a master. "Surely your God is the God of gods," he declared, "and the Lord of kings and a revealer of mysteries, for you were able to reveal this mystery."

Nebuchadnezzar had always thought of Marduk as the supreme god. But One higher than Marduk had revealed Himself, and the king acknowledged Him as "God of gods" and "Lord of kings."

The Babylonian ruler appointed Daniel chief prefect, a position that allowed authority over the other counselors. Daniel's three friends also received important positions.

Great rejoicing swept through the once-condemned counselors and their families as they left the prison courtyard after nearly 36 hours of detention. Their homes lay in ruins, but they owed their lives to their new leader, Belteshazzar (Daniel)—a man of wisdom, and servant of the Most High God.

---

[1] Much of the dialogue used in this chapter has been taken from Daniel 2.
[2] Daniel 2:21-23.

Chapter 6

A Donkey
Brays His Last

"We don't have enough men!" Nebuchadnezzar yelled to his officers. "Retreat, or Egypt will annihilate us!" The young king cursed his gods. The bulk of his army fought elsewhere, and without them he had no hope of winning this battle.

During the days that followed, Pharaoh struggled to ensnare and destroy his enemy, but Nebuchadnezzar's zigzagging remnants eluded him. Crossing the ford at Carchemish, the Babylonians won and lost all at once. They escaped destruction, but forfeited control of Palestine.

"You fought well," Nebuchadnezzar consoled his soldiers as he rode along the lines. "Go home now. Rest awhile. We will avenge our dead another time." But he knew it would be years before he could take on Egypt again. Losses had been heavy on both sides, but his chariots had been wrecked, his horses slaughtered, and the lion's share of his seasoned infantry slain.

Jehoiakim rejoiced when Pharaoh drove Nebuchadnezzar from Palestine. "Go home immediately," he ordered the Babylonian ambassador, "or I'll turn you over to Egypt as a spy."

"I'll go," the envoy said as he bowed politely. "But if you stop paying tribute, Nebuchadnezzar will punish you when he returns—"

"He's not coming back!" the Judahite king shouted. "Guards! Throw him out!"

The Egyptian diplomat entered Jehoiakim's large palace just as the guards escorted the Babylonian from the king's presence. "Ah, Your Majesty," he cooed, "I admire your new palace. Reminds me of Pharaoh's own."

"I'm glad you like it," the king nodded. He had drained the palace treasury and enslaved many of his people to build the enormous cedar structure. Jeremiah warned of God's sure judgments for such abuses, and the enraged public loathed both the building and its maker.

"I see you have smoothed the road for the lord of the Nile." The ambassador swept his hand toward the southwest.

"Yes." Jehoiakim seemed pleased with himself. "We have broken ties with Babylon and want to reunite with Egypt."

The ambassador could not hide his delight. "Your return will delight Pharaoh, for he fought this war to get you back."

"He will not be half as happy as I." Jehoiakim not only considered Egypt less oppressive than Nebuchadnezzar, but identified himself with Pharaoh's adventurism. "But Babylon may return," he added. "Will you help us?"

"All that we can."

"Curse those Babylonians!" Jehoiakim exploded.

Several years had passed since Nebuchadnezzar had left Palestine.

"Those desert marauders aren't Babylonians," the prime minister corrected for the fourth time.

"I know, I know! But Nebuchadnezzar instigates and supports them." The Judahite king hated the time-serving courtiers who surrounded him, and they regarded him with equal disdain.

If only I could find able men that I could trust, he thought, *I'd replace these fools.* But he had executed or exiled everyone of any moral worth, and he didn't even realize what he'd done.

"We've tried to stop them," the general mumbled, gritting his teeth. "As soon as we learn of a raid, we race to confront them. But by then the raiders have already gone, and—"

"—taken scores of captives with them," the chamberlain interrupted, pacing the floor. His official title, "cupbearer," arose from his duty of tasting the king's wine for poison. But this position of trust also made him prime minister and intercessor between the people and their king. "We've lost hundreds of people."

"To say nothing of gold, silver, livestock, and food." The king chafed at the material losses more than the human misery.

"Why don't we ask Egypt for help?" the general suggested. "They promised aid."

"We could." The king stared out the window. "But there couldn't be more than a few hundred raiders"—he turned again to the council—"and we should be able to defend ourselves against them. If we called on Egypt, all the world would think we're helpless."

"Then let's station more men in the towns," the general said. "Catch them before they strike."

"Fine." The king's voice wore a razor edge. "But maintain a strong defense in Jerusalem."

"We'll be careful," the general sighed.

But the raids continued, destroying towns, killing and capturing people and livestock, carting all valuables to the bandits' desert lairs. The army launched numerous preemptive raids, but even after several years they didn't prevent a single attack.

People in the towns suffered terribly, and unrest blossomed

on every side. "If the army can't protect us from desert bandits," they protested, "how can they stop major invasions?"

❁❁

"It's time we took back Hatti-land [Palestine]," Nebuchadnezzar announced to his chamberlain one day during a feast in the palace. "Our merchants need protection from Egyptian harassment."

The chamberlain nodded as he listened to his favorite song:

> "O Babylon,
> whosoever beholds thee is filled with rejoicing,
> whosoever dwells in Babylon increases his life,
> Whosoever speaks evil of Babylon
> is like one who kills his own mother;
> Babylon is like a sweet date palm,
> whose fruit is lovely to behold."

When the song ended, Nebuchadnezzar spoke again. "If that donkey Jehoiakim were as faithful to his God as Belteshazzar is, he'd keep his pledge. Save us a lot of trouble." Acrobats cavorted into the courtyard, momentarily distracting the king's attention.

Preparation for the campaign occupied Nebuchadnezzar for weeks. And many more weeks passed before he stood again on Palestinian soil. It had been eight years since the second Carchemish encounter.

As he advanced, he followed an old Assyrian strategy: he subdued every rebellious city-state in turn, leaving his major opponents without any nearby allies when he at last unleashed his power on them.

Within weeks of crossing the Euphrates, Nebuchadnezzar approached Jerusalem. The world's most efficient war machine had more than overwhelmed any resistance. And scouts informed him of all its movements.

As the enemy forces surrounded the Judahite capital, the king secretly called a few top officials to decide the nation's fate. Should they resist—or surrender?

"Surrender?" the general protested. "Not without a fight. We're not helpless, you know."

"We'll provoke them if we resist," the prime minister objected. "Then when we *do* surrender, many people will die."

"Why fight at all?" Jehoiakim, his anger growing with his frustration, fumed. "Our armies have floundered before desert rats for eight years. Why rattle our weapons now?"

"You know how swiftly those raiders move," the general barked, raising his chin in disdain.

"I know! I know! And I've also seen the speed with which you move your military snails! I've never seen such incompetence in my life!" He gritted his teeth as he spat out the words. "And you want to fight Nebuchadnezzar? If he doesn't skin you alive, I will!"

Shocked silence filled the chamber as Jehoiakim stalked about the room, jaw set, arms folded, defiance emanating from every pore. "Surrender is our only hope." The king's voice sounded quieter, but had lost none of its hostility. "Nebuchadnezzar treated us fairly before. Perhaps he'll favor us again."

"Fool!" the general roared.

"Silence, you shield-pounder!" The king whirled around, whipping out his sword as he faced the commander. "Get out of my sight!"

The fuming soldier slipped from the room, mumbling to himself. "We'll see who surrenders . . . I still command the troops!"

The other counselors withdrew, distraught at the king's tantrum. Jehoiakim shrugged and summoned a scribe, dictating to him a surrender note: "We have no desire to fight," he wrote. "We will open our gates as we did before. Please treat us with mercy."

After dispatching a courier to lower the message over the wall, the king resumed his place on his throne. Anger and uncertainty gnawed at his stomach. *Surrender is no embarrassment,* he thought, *for victory's impossible. But for a general to publicly humiliate me—unthinkable!*

"I must replace that man," he growled when his prime minister returned. "Well, not just now—perhaps after Babylon leaves."

Nebuchadnezzar smiled as his scribe translated Jehoiakim's message. He'd expected to spend several months subduing Jerusalem. But it seemed that Judah's treacherous king lacked the bravery to back up his boasting. He'd given up without a fight.

"I see no reason we can't grant his request," the king chuckled to his general. "They gave us no trouble last time."

"Maybe," the commander said cautiously. "But it could be a trap."

"Then be on guard." Nebuchadnezzar summoned a scribe to write his acceptance. "Have a unit ready to capture the king if anything goes wrong. Bring him to me if you take him alive."

Jehoiakim received Nebuchadnezzar's answer within an hour of his request: "Surrender accepted. Meet my delegation at the East Gate." Nebuchadnezzar's seal graced the message on the piece of broken pottery.

Flanked by his handpicked bodyguard, the Judahite king led his officials. The streets lay empty, but the walls above the entrance bristled with armed men. The king, focusing on the gate, failed to notice that every archer had an arrow in his bow.

The procession paused as the great cedar doors swung inward on their massive stone sockets. He eyed the multitude outside, waiting behind the official entourage.

The royal party stood some distance inside the gate while the Babylonians began their wary advance. As the envoys neared, Jehoiakim began to kneel, as custom demanded.

Suddenly, arrows cascaded from the walls! Ambush!

Swept by panic, Jehoiakim realized that he had no sword! Terrified, he fled, leaving most of his bodyguard to be hacked to death. Hundreds of Babylonian soldiers charged through the gates, killing everyone they encountered.

Jehoiakim raced through the streets, seeking a place to hide. The Babylonians quickly butchered his surviving guards and cornered him in a dead-end street. Cruel hands shackled him in iron, jerking him about. He gasped for mercy as they dragged him back the way he'd come, but they ignored his cries.

They hadn't gone far before they realized that their royal prisoner was dead. Altering course, they dragged his lifeless body through the Dung Gate to the Hinnom Valley—the city dump. Below lay rotting carcasses and bleached skeletons of countless animals—discarded for birds and wild dogs to devour. The Babylonians tossed the still-shackled royal corpse onto the putrid pile, did an about-face, and returned to the city.

Jehoiakim had died at age 36. He had ruled Judah for 11 years.

❧❧

Nebuchadnezzar placed Jehoiakim's 18-year-old son on the throne of Judah while he continued his Palestinian campaign.

"I'm not sure I can trust Jehoiachin," he commented to his general. The king had abandoned his chariot for exercise on his favorite white stallion.

"Why not?"

"He hates me for the death of his father." Nebuchadnezzar studied the troops as they marched toward Gaza. "One of my spies overheard him say, 'Wait till Babylon leaves—we'll seek aid from Egypt.'"

"He said that?"

"According to our agent, his exact words."

The general ran his hands through his hair. "What will you do?"

"I can't leave him in charge." Nebuchadnezzar stared at the distant walls of Gaza, now visible from his vantage point. "I wish I had another Belteshazzar here."

They descended the rise and crossed a dry riverbed, keeping abreast of the infantry. The king scratched his chin through his curly black beard and shrugged. "I suppose Jehoiakim's younger brother Mattaniah could do the job."

So when Nebuchadnezzar returned to Jerusalem three months later, he sent Jehoiachin and his family to Babylon, crowning instead his 21-year-old uncle Mattaniah.

"Your name shall no longer be Mattaniah," Nebuchadnezzar announced, "but Zedekiah—'Yahweh is righteousness.' Let that be a continual reminder that you've pledged loyalty to me in Yahweh's name."

Chapter 7

Trial by Fire

For a while after Daniel had interpreted the king's dream, Nebuchadnezzar had showed respect for Yahweh, God of Judah. But his ambition for greatness soon distracted him from his worship of Daniel's God, and he returned to his Babylonian deities. His counselors, uncomfortable with his interest in the Jewish God, came up with a ploy to strengthen his loyalty to the native gods.

"O king, live forever," one of them intoned one day. "Your servants enjoy great prosperity because you are our king. We desire to display our gratitude on your next birthday."

"Continue."

"If it please my lord, we will erect a statue in your likeness so all will know of our loyalty to you."

"It pleases me," Nebuchadnezzar replied, remembering the image he had seen in the dream. Daniel's words "You are the head of gold" still rang in his mind. "Do all that you have in mind."

"My lord," another counselor said, "why don't we overlay the statue with gold, silver, brass, and iron—like the one in your dream?"

"Yes, my lord," added another. "Belteshazzar's God made you the head of gold. Why not celebrate the dream and your exalted place as head of the image?"

Nebuchadnezzar gazed at the patterns on the wall of the courtyard. The dream had impressed him. But to be just the head?

His empire had expanded, now stretching from the Persian Gulf to the Mediterranean Sea. Captured artisans from many cultures now made Babylon the most beautiful city in the world, and its king had become respected everywhere for his learning, wisdom, and statesmanship. His achievements often overshadowed his interest in Daniel's God, and at times he had forgotten Him altogether.

"The dream . . . a great revelation, of course," he continued. His eyes narrowed, his jaw tensed. "And Belteshazzar's interpretation—remarkable. But the dream makes me only the head. I don't want to be just the head. I want to be the whole image!"

The counselors smiled to themselves. They had been happy to benefit from the instruction that God had given through Daniel. But they saw Nebuchadnezzar's fascination with the God of Judah as a threat to their own position and power, and they feared that Belteshazzar's influence could eventually eclipse their own.

"Of course, my lord," the oldest counselor agreed. "You are the greatest king who ever lived. You are the entire image."

Nebuchadnezzar smiled. "Then let's overlay the entire image with . . . *gold*." He measured each word with care. "And let's use this as an opportunity for all nations to declare their loyalty to me. The greatest king who will *ever* live on earth. Babylon *will exist forever!*"

⁂

"Tell me about Judah," Nebuchadnezzar questioned his chief intelligence officer.

"The news is not good, my lord."

"Oh?" The king frowned.

"Your servant received a report from our agent in Jerusalem only yesterday, my lord. A certain prophet of their religion, one Hananiah by name—"

"Our Shadrach?"

"No. The name Hananiah seems common among the Jews." The man rubbed his chin. "A while ago Hananiah spoke in the Temple, my lord, saying that Babylon would be destroyed and that all Judahite captives would be free in two years."

"The swine should die!"

"That's not all, my lord. Another prophet named Jeremiah rebuked him in front of a large crowd—called him a liar, and said the captivity would last 70 years. In fact, my lord," the officer grinned, "he said the king of Babylon is, in his words, 'God's servant to punish the Jews for their unfaithfulness to Yahweh.'"

"He said that?"

"Yes, my lord."

"I like that man Jeremiah." The king smiled. "It takes courage to say that in front of all those people." He chuckled. "So I'm God's servant, eh? Tell me more."

"Well, my lord, things got a little nasty for a few minutes. Hananiah labeled Jeremiah a liar and threatened to kill him. But then . . ." The officer paused.

"What happened?"

"Jeremiah said, 'Thus says Yahweh: "Behold, Hananiah, I will cast *you* off the face of the earth. This very year you will die because you have fostered rebellion among My people.'" My lord, Hananiah became very frightened and left the Temple."

"Lost his nerve?"

"Apparently. But here's the most interesting part of all this."

"Oh?"

"Less than two months later Hananiah dropped dead."

"H'mmm. I need to know more about this Jeremiah. He reminds me somewhat of Belteshazzar."

Nebuchadnezzar gazed into the distance for several minutes, considering the different Jews he'd known. Some had outstanding characters—Belteshazzar, his friends, and now Jeremiah. Their fidelity had for a time tempted him to abandon Babylon's many conflicting deities in favor of the one God who could produce stalwart men like that. But then the treachery of Jehoiakim, Hananiah, and others who claimed to serve Yahweh flashed before his mind, and he dismissed the idea.

"How goes it with King Zedekiah?"

"Not so well, my lord." Nebuchadnezzar frowned as the officer continued. "The man cannot be trusted. He promised to serve Babylon, but after you left he became involved in local alliances. His counselors have almost talked him into forming a 'league of mutual assistance' with Egypt."

"What!" The king rose from his throne and paced the courtyard for several minutes. "I'll have to do something about him." He scratched his head. "I know! That statue for my birthday—a good opportunity for national leaders to reaffirm their loyalty. I want Zedekiah and his counselors here for the dedication. That ought to impress them with the importance of keeping their oath with me."

Black smoke billowed skyward from cone-shaped brick kilns surrounding the uncompleted structure. Bricks still in the furnaces glowed as laborers stoked fires to assure that they reached their proper temperature.

The colossal likeness of Nebuchadnezzar had been several months in the making, its head rising 90 feet above the Shinar plain, its feet firmly planted on a pedestal 45 feet high. Scaffolding surrounded the statue as craftsmen overlaid its entire surface with thin sheets of gold. They would use four tons of the yellow metal before completion. Still others built a raised platform from which the king would receive his birthday honors, and lower stages for musicians, priests, and guards.

Already, heads of state from the various territories had begun arriving, sightseeing and preparing themselves for the festivities.

"What will we do?" Mishael asked one day. "Our positions require that we attend. And you realize that they'll want us to bow before that idol."

Hananiah put his hand on the younger man's shoulder. "We cannot bow, Mishael; you know that."

"I know." His face showed the strain of his mental anguish. "But there'll be trouble if we refuse."

"No doubt!"

"I wish Daniel were here." Azariah had been even quieter than usual. "He always encouraged us during difficult times."

"But he's not here," Hananiah replied, "and he won't be back for several months. We'll have to trust Yahweh to see us through this one by ourselves."

⁂

"I've never seen so many people," Mishael whispered as the three friends took their assigned places near the feet of the golden image.

"Nor I," returned Azariah. "It's as though the whole world has come to pay homage to Nebuchadnezzar."

A trumpet sounded.

"Hush," Hananiah cautioned. "The royal party is arriving."

"Remember our agreement," Mishael reminded.

A wave of motion swept over the crowd as all bowed in respect to their king. Nebuchadnezzar extended his golden scepter, and then seated himself under an ornate canopy. A hiss of whispers arose and then faded as a herald stepped forward on a lower platform.

"This is what you are commanded to do, O peoples, nations, and men of every language." The herald did not shout, but his cultured voice carried over that immense throng. He paused as others translated his message into several different languages.

Then he continued. "As soon as you hear the sound of the horn, flute, zither, lyre, harp, pipes, and all kinds of music, you must fall down and worship the image of gold that King Nebuchadnezzar has set up."[1] The command wafted about in several tongues before fading into the distance. No one objected, but the man had not finished.

"Whoever does not fall down and worship will immediately be thrown into a blazing furnace." The official turned and bowed to the king as the translators finished their task.

Hananiah glanced at the others and smiled grimly. Their moment of truth had come. In the past they had chosen to obey God in many minor ways, but now they were laying their lives on the line. And yet they felt no fear, no regrets. They had chosen to trust in Him, and now He had granted them perfect peace.

The chief musician raised his hands, and music floated into the air. Thousands of human beings sank to their knees, their foreheads touching the ground.

A smile flickered across Nebuchadnezzar's face. Nowhere in all that crowd could he see anyone still stan—

What! Near the front three men remained upright, challenging the command of the greatest king of all time.

A rustle fluttered among the prostrate forms, and thousands of eyes peered at three men who must have lost their senses.

"O king, live forever." The voice caused all heads to pivot toward the royal platform. A group of astrologers had come with news the king already knew. It had long angered them that foreigners had been elevated to equality with them. Now they saw a chance to get even. "There are some Jews whom you have set over the affairs of the province of Babylon—

Shadrach, Meshach, and Abednego—who pay no attention to you, O king," they announced. "They neither serve your gods nor worship the image of gold you have set up."

Nebuchadnezzar's face changed several shades as he gazed at the standing individuals—three young men whom he had favored above so many others. "Bring them to me," he ordered, and within minutes they had been escorted before the king.

Nebuchadnezzar came right to the point. "Is it true, Shadrach, Meshach, and Abednego, that you do not serve my gods or worship the image of gold I have set up?"

Certain of their answer, a wave of panic mushroomed within the king's stomach. Their apparent lack of fear unnerved him, reminding him of Belteshazzar. He had sent Daniel away, knowing he would refuse to bow to a golden idol. But alas, he had forgotten the three friends!

Recognizing their intense loyalty to him as well as to their God, he valued the men. But he had bricked himself into a corner. Now he saw no way out but their giving in— just this once. After all, he had honored them, raised them from slavery to royal service. Did he expect too much to hope that they would help him save face—*just this once?*

Give them one more chance! He told himself.

"Now when you hear the sound of the music"—his voice carried across the throng—"if you are ready to fall down and worship the image I made, very good. But if you do not worship it, you will be thrown immediately into a blazing furnace."

The king's authoritative tone swayed even himself, bolstering his pride and distorting his reasoning. What began as a plea for their support became a blatant boast. Rising from his throne, he clenched his fist and shouted at the sky. "Then what god will be able to rescue you from my hand?"

Dressed in expensive robes, wearing a bejeweled crown

worth a fortune; surrounded by fabulous wealth, hundreds of servants, and the greatest men of the world; and standing before the grandest statue ever built, Nebuchadnezzar made an awesome spectacle.

Meshach's eyes met those of the angry monarch. The young Jew's trust in God had helped him conquer his earlier timidity. "O Nebuchadnezzar," his calm but forceful words carried to most of the crowd. "We do not need to defend ourselves before you in this matter. If we are thrown into the blazing furnace, the God we serve is able to save us from it, and He will rescue us from your hand, O king."

Nebuchadnezzar couldn't believe his ears. A god who could save them from fire? Rescue them from *his* hand?

"But even if He does not," Meshach continued, "we want you to know, O king, that we *will not* serve your gods or worship the image of gold you have set up." The young man bowed in courtesy and then remained standing erect before the king.

The king's mind reeled. What courage! What dedication! *What treachery!*

He had been tolerant of their religion, for it had caused his government no problems. But now they had publicly dis-obeyed a direct order—an insult to his authority and an act of rebellion against his government. Anger erupted with the force of a volcano. "You ungrateful swine!" he shouted. "I'll roast you alive!"

"Arioch!" he shouted to his executioner, who stood not 10 feet away. "Heat that furnace"—he pointed to a nearby brick kiln—"seven times hotter." The king sensed that he faced more than ordinary men, and he needed to use more than ordinary force. "Bind these three and have your strongest men throw them into the fire. We'll see what be-comes of their blasphemy against our gods."

Arioch's men, feeling the urgency in Nebuchadnezzar's

voice, rushed toward the three Jews. Throwing them to the ground, they began tying their hands and feet.

Hananiah quoted Scripture, his voice unsteady because of the rough treatment he received from the guards: "'When you pass through the waters, I will be with you.'" Mishael and Azariah joined him. "'And when you pass through the rivers, they will not sweep over you. When you walk through the fire, you will not be burned; the flames will not set you ablaze. For I am the Lord, your God, the Holy One of Israel, your Savior.'"[2]

While strong hands bound the offenders, others tossed handfuls of an asphalt-and-straw mixture into the kiln. Within minutes the bricks lining the opening began to glow cherry-red. By the time the three Hebrews had been carried to the oven, the color had turned to white. Flames and black smoke billowed from the top of the kiln.

Those stoking the fire backed away from the furnace as the heat increased, but they continued to toss in more fuel as long as they could heave it through the opening.

Pairs of royal guards, carrying the young victims by the feet and shoulders, steeled themselves to the intense heat as they hurled the bodies through the opening. The crowd watched in horror as the soldiers, overcome by the blast of heat issuing from the furnace, stumbled and fell, grew lobster-red, and blistered—roasted to death in front of the oven.

What must have been the fate of those cast into the fire! Nebuchadnezzar expected loyalty, they realized. Disobedience would bring a ghastly fate!

The king sank back onto his throne, drained. What had he done! In a fit of anger he had destroyed three young men and lost six of his most loyal guards. Numbly he stared into the fire.

If he could only reverse the events of the past few minutes . . .

He wished that he'd never built the image, never sought to test the loyalty of his subjects. It had all turned out wrong.

But his thoughts suddenly froze as he gazed into the furnace. "What's that?" he shouted, leaping to his feet, eyes fixed on the fiery opening to the kiln. Had he imagined it? "Wasn't it three men that we tied up and threw into the fire?" he gasped, the color draining from his face.

"Certainly, O king," replied his chamberlain.

"But look!" Nebuchadnezzar exclaimed, forgetting the multitudes. "Look! I see four men walking around in the fire, unbound and unharmed."

Others saw it too, despite the glare of the flames. But how could anyone survive such searing heat? And who was the fourth man?

The king trembled with fear as words, unbidden, escaped his lips. "The fourth is like the Son of God."[3]

Shame flooded Nebuchadnezzar. Forgetting his dignity, he bounded down the stairway and through the crowd. He approached the furnace as near as its heat would allow. "Shadrach! Meshach! Abednego!" he called. "Servants of the Most High God, come out! Come here!"

The three young men had remained in the furnace in obedience to their king's command. But now they stepped through the opening of the white-hot kiln and out of the fire—unimpeded, for the ropes had vaporized in the blaze.

The curious multitudes surged forward and surrounded them, touching them, sniffing their clothing. Not a burn mark or singed hair could be seen; not a trace of smoke could they smell.

The king could not contain his astonishment. His joy knew no bounds. The tension of the past hour and the growing recognition of the power of the God of heaven had exhausted him.

The great golden image, constructed at such lavish expense and effort, had been so important to Nebuchadnezzar a few minutes before that the lives of his most trusted servants meant nothing by comparison. But all that had been forgotten in the light of the glory he had seen shining from the fiery furnace. Tears of relief ran down his cheeks as he hugged all three of his friends at once. He could keep quiet no longer.

"Praise be to the God of Shadrach, Meshach, and Abednego," he shouted, turning from side to side so that all could hear. "He sent His angel and rescued His servants! They trusted in Him, defying even the king's command, and were willing to give up their lives rather than serve or worship any god except their own.

"Therefore." He summoned a scribe to record his words. "Therefore, I decree that the people of any nation or language who say anything against the God of Shadrach, Meshach, and Abednego"—Nebuchadnezzar's love of the sound of his voice and pride in his power began to carry him away again—"they will be cut into pieces and their houses be turned into piles of rubble, for no other god can save in this way."

---

[1] Portions of this chapter have been quoted from Daniel 3.
[2] Isaiah 43:2, 3.
[3] Daniel 3:25, KJV.

Chapter 8

Almost Persuaded

"Swear in Yahweh's name," Nebuchadnezzar demanded. "Then I know you'll be faithful to me."

Before returning home, the king of Judah bowed before Babylon's golden throne to assure the great king of his abiding loyalty. Nebuchadnezzar knew of Daniel's fidelity to the God of heaven, and he reasoned that Zedekiah would also respect an oath in the holy name.

But the religion of Yahweh meant nothing to Judah's monarch, for to him it merely provided a means by which to advance his political position. So he saw no conflict between an oath in Yahweh's name and his obeisance to a golden image.

In fact, the refusal of the three Jewish exiles to bow before the huge idol had irritated him, for such an act caused him public embarrassment. Their unreasoning dedication to Yahweh made no sense to him, and he had been as surprised as anyone by their miraculous escape.

He had become even more galled over Nebuchadnezzar's insistence that he add a new member to his inner circle. "This new advisor," ordered Nebuchadnezzar, "shall be the prophet Jeremiah. Listen to that man, Zedekiah. He can save you a lot of trouble."

Many exiles from Judah had settled in a small town on the Chebar Canal, southwest of Babylon. This waterway, an irrigation canal, ran almost 200 miles from north of Sippar to south of Uruk. At first the Jews had been slaves, working the land around the small farming community. But Babylonian policy allowed slaves to earn their freedom, and in time most became free.

They worked hard, and often went without things others considered necessities, in order to improve their lot. In time they built houses, bought small plots for gardens, or set up their own private businesses. Before many years had passed, most reached an economic level equal to, and sometimes exceeding, that of their Babylonian neighbors.

In spite of their prosperity, they became discouraged. Feeling that God had forsaken them, some broke with traditional ways, mingled with the Babylonians, and intermarried. Many abandoned their heritage altogether.

Ezekiel and other leaders sought to prevent this and to preserve their identity. They taught faithful Sabbath observance, circumcised their male infants, and encouraged people to practice the traditions of the fathers.

In spite of this, problems developed. Many grew tired of the drab flatness of Mesopotamia and became homesick for the hills of Judah. Rumors of an early return plagued the settlement, and frustrated young people sometimes clashed with the Babylonian authorities.

News of Hananiah's predictions in Jerusalem stirred up old hatreds and fostered discontent. Zealous to lead their people back home, two local leaders named Ahab and Zedekiah promoted the false prophecies. Although they became involved in numerous adulterous affairs, their talk of imminent return to Judah made them popular, and many overlooked their behavior while accepting their message.

While King Zedekiah stayed in Babylon, his scribe, Seraiah, visited the settlement of exiles on the Chebar. He gathered the community leaders on the riverbank, together with a small crowd, and read Jeremiah's scroll—against the vigorous objections of the false prophets.

"To the Jews in Babylon," the scribe began. "Build homes, raise families, establish businesses, plant vineyards, because most of you will spend the rest of your lives there. Don't listen to those who say the captivity will end soon, for such lies will only bring you trouble."

Finished, Seraiah tied the scroll to a large rock and threw it into the river, as Jeremiah had instructed. Then he kissed Ezekiel and other friendly leaders goodbye and rejoined King Zedekiah in Babylon.

"Daniel!" Mishael exclaimed as he burst into the room. "Those two false prophets of Chebar, Ahab and Zedekiah, have been executed—roasted in a fire!"

"Oh, no!" Daniel had returned from his special mission and had been rejoicing with Hananiah and Azariah over their deliverance from the fiery furnace. Tears welled up in his eyes. "They could have been a blessing to our people."

"If they had only listened to Jeremiah's letter," Azariah groaned. "He told them that the captivity would last for 70 years. And yet they insisted that our people would go home in two."

"They were no doubt led astray by that false prophet Hananiah," Mishael said. "Even though he died (just as Jeremiah had predicted), many people still believed him. I guess it's because he preached what they wanted to hear."

"And it created havoc among our people here," Daniel added. "I received several reports of how they refused to work or cooperate with the authorities. In some places the resistance and disorder they caused led to death and injuries."

"All because of the false testimony of two self-appointed prophets," Azariah sighed.

"Too bad," Hananiah said. "But things should become quieter now that they've been punished."

Daniel put a hand on his friend's arm. "Let's hope and pray that you're right."

❧❧

When King Zedekiah and his escort returned to Jerusalem, they found a gathering of ambassadors from several Palestinian nations at the palace.

"We despise the oppression of Babylon," an envoy from Edom announced, bowing to show his respect for Judah's ruler. "We far prefer that Egypt coordinate our affairs."

"Yes," joined in the Ammonite ambassador. "Pharaoh taxes us, but he doesn't drag our people to Egypt."

"He does if we refuse to pay our taxes," the Moabite chided, spoiling for an argument with his traditional enemy.

"True," the Ammonite grunted, sidestepping the bait. "But not from general policy like Nebuchadnezzar. If we would all unite with Egypt, I believe Babylon would leave us alone."

"That's right," agreed the delegate from Tyre. "And if you'll remember, Egypt has mauled Babylon several times. If we had only supported the Egyptians then, they might have destroyed the Mesopotamian lion altogether."

"You embarrass me." Zedekiah held up his hands, trying to stop them. "I've just returned from Babylon. I took an oath to remain loyal to Nebuchadnezzar."

"So what!" laughed the Sidonian ambassador. "You needn't fear to break your word. We'll all protect each other."

"I wish I could believe that," Zedekiah scowled, "but it does sound good." The king of Judah often wavered between opposite opinions, never able to make up his mind for himself. In fact, he had at times allowed one group of advisors to draft official policies while permitting another clique to revise them. Friends and enemies alike pushed him this way and that, despising him, using him—and yet fearing to trust his word.

"Our alliance will work." The Edomite smiled, seeking to bury old hatreds. "Pharaoh has promised to protect us—with his full army, if need be. We have nothing to fear."

At that precise moment Jeremiah entered the room and began handing small wooden objects to the ambassadors. At first the men thought they were gifts from Zedekiah, but one look at his furious face banished that idea.

"These are yokes, gentlemen." Jeremiah smiled as he adjusted one worn around his own neck so that it rode at the proper angle. "Wear them the way I'm wearing mine. Please accept these as gifts from Yahweh to your kings." He laid one in Zedekiah's lap. "Yahweh says: 'I made the earth, the sea, the heavens, and every beast in them. I have the power to do whatever I wish with all these things, and to give them to whomever I choose.

"'I have given the earth and everyone on it to Nebuchadnezzar and his successors. All nations will serve him. Someday I will destroy Babylon, but until then, every nation who refuses to submit to her yoke will die by sword, famine, and pestilence. Yet those who wear Babylon's yoke will remain in their own lands.

"'Do not listen to anyone who tells you to resist, for I have spoken,' says Yahweh, 'and I will cause it to happen.'"

"These will make interesting souvenirs," the Ammonite said after Jeremiah left the room. "But I have no intention of serving Babylon."

"Nor do I," Zedekiah agreed as he tossed his miniature yoke away.

"Gentlemen," announced the Moabite as he broke his yoke over his knee. "Let us form an alliance against Babylon."

When news of Zedekiah's rebellion reached Nebuchadnezzar, he flew into a rage. "That Jewish swine!" he shouted as his servants backed away. "Less than a year since he promised me in the name of Yahweh, his God. He vowed he would serve me all the days of his life. Doesn't his word, or his God, mean anything to him?"

"I don't understand those Jews," Nebuchadnezzar later sputtered to his chamberlain. "Belteshazzar and his friends are above reproach. Would that I had the peace that they have—the surety that I pleased my god."

The king scratched the side of his face. Streaks of gray highlighted his curly black beard, and worry lines creased his forehead. He had ruled for 15 years, built scores of beautiful and costly buildings, and enlarged the city until it spread over 12 square miles. Visitors regarded his hanging gardens as an architectural marvel.

And yet Judah had become a recurring nightmare. Nebuchadnezzar had exerted every effort to maintain peace within the embrace of Babylon. He needed them, their strategic location, their craftspeople, their taxes.

"Ezekiel and Jeremiah—the prophets. One here and one in Jerusalem. What courage to stand up against their own people. I've heard reports of their sermons. They sound much like our Belteshazzar."

As the monarch ran his fingers through his hair, he considered the Jews that he'd known. "At times I've been impressed by Belteshazzar and his friends. Their God seemed attractive. What I wouldn't give to have the peace and courage they have! What a powerful deity—He saved them from fire!

"But—" The king examined the patterns on the opposite wall, as awe melted into anger. "But Jehoiakim and Zedekiah! Those scoundrels worshipped the same God—and it did nothing for them. They refused to honor oaths made in their deity's name! And those so-called prophets—what are their names?"

The chamberlain had come out of his corner. "I believe you speak of Hananiah of Jerusalem, and Ahab and Zedekiah of the Chebar settlement, my lord."

"Yes, yes. Prophets! Do they also speak for Belteshazzar's God? They've caused us nothing but trouble." Nebuchadnezzar shook his head. "What kind of God produces such opposite personalities among those who serve Him?"

The chamberlain, accustomed to the king's lectures, smiled and nodded his head as the Babylonian ruler continued.

"Now, our gods—they have good points and bad points. We expect that our people will have good points and bad points too. But this Jewish God—He has only a good side. Belteshazzar and Jeremiah—they seem only good too. But the others?"

The king sat down on his throne and put his head in his hands. "I'm not sure I like that kind of deity. I prefer ours. They always seem angry—demand impossible things—but at least we know where we stand."

Thoughtfully he stroked his beard. "They say that 'you know a god by the people who serve him.' If all Jews were like Belteshazzar and Jeremiah, I'd gladly worship their God. But—oh, I don't know."

Chapter 9

Crushing the Revolt

"That double-crosser!" Nebuchadnezzar raged. "Zedekiah's done it again! Stopped paying tribute—expelled my ambassador—"

"It does look serious," his chamberlain agreed.

"I need Hatti-land. My best trading routes pass their way. My people pay double taxes to Pharaoh, and all because the king of Judah resists my authority."

"What will you do?"

Nebuchadnezzar scratched his head. "I'll—" He winced, then declared, "I'll crush them. Destroy their cities—transplant the survivors someplace else."

"Rather harsh measures." Because of his trusted position (tasting the king's wine for poison), he could offer more realistic counsel than those whose jobs depended upon pleasing the king.

The king frowned. "Yes. But those Jews have pestered me ever since my ascension—and I've done everything to keep them on my side. I even have a Jewish counselor."

"Belteshazzar?"

"Yes. A good man, too. Always dependable. If all his people were like him . . ." His voice trailed into silence.

Thousands gathered on the plains around Babylon as Nebuchadnezzar planned the Hatti-land campaign. Many brought wives or female servants, and each carried an assortment of his favorite weapons—battle axes, swords of all sizes and shapes, leather shields, battle bows, javelins, slings.

Through the weeks of preparation the king himself directed the organization and training. In time the ragged bands of brigands, farmers, artisans, adventurers, and professional soldiers melded into an efficient military machine.

Then came the day that all plans had been laid, all supplies gathered and packed into thousands of waiting wagons, and all goodbyes said. The monstrous army waited only for the order to march.

Nebuchadnezzar smiled at his attaché. "Time to move."

Trumpets sounded the advance, and leaders shouted commands to endless lines of soldiers. The seething, multinational mass of men began its northwestward trek along the Euphrates. Hundreds of thousands of marching feet, prancing hooves, and chariot and freight wagon wheels produced a rumble that could be heard for miles. On windless days this horde stirred clouds of dust that drifted high into the air.

Nebuchadnezzar knew that such an army could not approach anyone unaware. "But who cares," he laughed. "No city or nation would dare resist me anyway."

❧❧

"We won't be victorious unless the gods are favorable," Nebuchadnezzar fretted to his chamberlain.

The royal cupbearer bowed. "I've summoned your astrologers and soothsayers, my lord."

"Very well." The king paced around his chariot, stopping at times to pat his white stallions and study the distant horizon. He stood at a fork in the road north of Damascus. One branch led to Jerusalem, while the other stretched toward Tyre and Sidon. While he wanted to terminate Zedekiah's revolt, that could be disastrous if the gods decreed some other course. Although he had already sought their will several times, he still wanted to be sure.

"Your advisors are here, my lord," the chamberlain announced a few minutes later.

"Good." Nebuchadnezzar turned to address them. The men claimed direct access to the gods who controlled Babylon's destiny. He had unmasked their deceptions at the time of his image dream. But that had been long ago, and his attitude toward them had shifted many times during the intervening years.

Each man carried a knapsack containing the tools with which he discovered the will of his god. The group seldom brought a unanimous report. But a simple majority was deemed sufficient for safe action—and each also knew Nebuchadnezzar's desire to punish Jerusalem.

"Gentlemen, shall we go to Jerusalem, or Tyre and Sidon?"

The counselors performed their rituals: one killed a goat and examined its liver for messages from his god. Another whirled a quiver of headless, tagged arrows around his head, until an arrow dislodged that revealed his god's decision. And still another examined the sunlight falling across an image of his god.

They compared results and reported to Nebuchadnezzar. Unanimous. "Advance toward Jerusalem—the gods will grant victory."

※※

"They're coming!" Terror spread as fast as gossip.

The Babylonian army swept from the north like an avalanche. Thousands of fierce soldiers swarmed over the hills and valleys around Jerusalem, bringing countless chariots and supply wagons, drawn by the most beautiful horses its inhabitants had ever seen.

Camps sprang up around the city as the army settled in for a long siege. A watchman spotted Nebuchadnezzar's chariot passing columns of men climbing the Mount of Olives—the best spot from which to observe the city. Messengers repeatedly came and went on errands. Later, when his bodyguard had erected a tent, the king disappeared into it.

The sun melted into the western horizon, and long shadows knit ragged patterns across the darkening landscape. The sky became a deep velvet as soldiers gathered around campfires to joke, sing, and discuss the coming siege. Countless fires flickered over hills and valleys. Distant ridges sparkled with night-watch beacons that blended with the spangled sky, making it difficult to determine where fires ended and stars began.

Night passed, and the campfires burned low. Dawn brought activity—but different from what the people of Jerusalem expected. Instead of bombarding soldiers on the walls with stones and arrows, the Babylonians hacked down every tree for miles and began constructing siege machines. Scouts studied gates, walls, and the city's defenders. Thousands of soldiers hauled baskets of dirt and rock to build a ramp against the wall, while dodging occasional projectiles from archers on the wall. The Babylonians carried oversized leather shields that arched over their heads, protecting them from incoming rocks and arrows.

For weeks Babylonians blocked every exit and all hope for help. Military engineers fabricated giant structures to weaken the city: wall-high towers from which archers could pick off its defenders; catapults to hurl rocks over the wall and destroy houses and people; battering rams on wheels.

When the soldiers had finished constructing the earthen ramp, they muscled a great wheeled ram up the incline and began swinging its giant blunt iron-tipped log against the upper, weaker portion of the wall.

Manning the ram was dangerous work. Jerusalem's defenders barraged those operating it with arrows and rocks to break their will and stop their work. The Babylonians tried to draw their attention away from the ram by lobbing arrows, fist-sized sling stones, and huge catapulted rocks onto and over the walls. Every person they killed weakened the city, because he or she could never be replaced.

The continual *whomp, whomp, whomp* of the ram against the wall measured the moments until the city died.

While the main force besieged Jerusalem, Nebuchadnezzar sent patrols out to ravage the countryside. They captured the smaller cities and towns, setting them all ablaze. In Lachish the fire became so intense that the limestone of the walls crumbled to dust.

Back in Jerusalem, everyone's heart grew faint. Because enemy hordes surrounded them, no supplies or recruits could enter the city. Few could deny that only a few months separated them from defeat or an agonizing death.

Zedekiah was no Hezekiah. Engrossed in personal affairs, he had spent little time preparing for the siege. Food warehouses stood half empty, and much of the grain had moldered. Many cisterns lay empty, and some harbored the putrid remains of animals. Hezekiah's tunnel had not been cleaned for years, and only a trickle ran through it.

The king couldn't have been less concerned, for the palace had plenty. "The Babylonians are bluffing," he scoffed. "They'll soon weary of trying to break through these strong walls and go somewhere else."

He had no idea of Nebuchadnezzar's persistence. So daily life in Jerusalem continued—as though no enemy surrounded the city at all.

But after several months Jerusalem began to feel the impact of the siege. Food and water became scarce, with no rationing to protect remaining supplies. The nobility, forced by a royal decree to free their slaves, now had to do their own work. Tempers flared. Fights, thefts, and murder became commonplace. Disease spread from house to house.

But without notice, the Babylonians suddenly vanished one day. Had they quit, or did they march to some distant war? No one knew. The once-teeming camp lay empty—save for tons of rubbish littering the countryside. Siege machines stood unmanned, and charred campfire rocks dotted the hillsides.

Delighted crowds ventured out to collect souvenirs. Self-appointed prophets predicted an early demise for Nebuchadnezzar, the release of Jehoiachin, and the return of the captives and their sacred Temple vessels.

The people discovered the reason for the disappearance of the Babylonians the following day. Reports of the approach of Pharaoh Hophra's army must have frightened the invaders away. Cheers filled Jerusalem. But they did not rejoice for any relief Yahweh had given them. Instead they proclaimed Pharaoh as the savior of Judah.

Jeremiah went to the Temple. "Nebuchadnezzar will return to destroy Jerusalem and the Temple," he told the priests. "We must not allow the ark to fall into their hands."

The high priest frowned at the mention of the Temple's destruction, but the prophet held up his hands. "Remember the first time he came?"

"Yes," the high priest grunted.

"He didn't destroy the city or the Temple then. But he did steal many sacred vessels."

The priest nodded, still bristling.

"Whether or not he destroys the Temple is not the issue, my friend." Jeremiah put his arm around the priest's shoulders, as though speaking to a close friend. "When Nebuchadnezzar returns, he'll surely take the remaining sacred vessels—including the ark of the covenant."

The priest sighed. "What should we do?"

"We must hide the ark where the Babylonians can't find it. Then when trouble passes, we'll return it to the Temple."

"All right." The high priest grimaced as he asked, "Will you help us?"

"Of course."

After dark, several priests, dressed in sackcloth, crept into the Temple. The high priest entered the Most Holy Place alone, covered the ark with a large cloth, pulled the veil aside, and whispered to the others. Four men backed into the sacred room, grasped the long poles protruding from the ark, and lifted it from the spot on which it had rested for centuries.

They tiptoed past the golden altar, the table of shewbread, the seven-branched candlestick, then slipped through the doorway, between the towering bronze pillars, and down the steps into the night. They had no idea that no one would ever see the sacred ark again.

༺༻

Death hung over Jerusalem. Nebuchadnezzar had beaten the Egyptians and returned to Judah's capital. Now, after months of fighting, the air reeked of raw sewage and decayed corpses.

Nebuchadnezzar surveyed the scene. "Only time stands between me and victory," he boasted. "Nothing can stop me now. And didn't the Jewish prophet Jeremiah call me 'God's servant to punish His disobedient people'?"

Nebuchadnezzar assigned the Jerusalem siege to his generals—Nergalsharezer of Sin-magir, Nebo-sarsechim the rabsaris, and Nergalsharezer the rab-mag. He outlined for them the procedures he expected them to follow in the final onslaught.

Then he withdrew with a sizable force to Riblah on the Orontes River, about 180 miles north of Judah. He wanted to lay plans for other Palestinian conquests before returning to Babylon.

Gate of the Gods

❧❧

The air had been still for days, and the sun glared down through cloudless summer skies. The people's skin, darkened from hunger and heat, often cracked open and developed oozing sores. Starvation snapped the minds of many. Mothers ate their own children. Others consumed the excrement of humans and animals.

The soldiers on the walls endured the most. Although starving and suffering from the blistering sun, they still strained every muscle to repel countless enemy attacks. Some dropped dead simply from exhaustion.

The day came when cascades of arrows crisscrossed between the siege tower and the city's defenders at Ephraim Gate. Scores fell on both sides as the battle escalated. Fighting had centered for hours on a breach in the wall made by the battering ram during the night.

But now, in the early-morning hours, walkways bridged tower and wall. Judah's bravest soldiers sprang forward to dislodge them, dying in a hail of arrows. A like fate befell the first Babylonians who sought to cross.

Jeremiah watched from the courtyard of the palace prison, where he had been incarcerated since hiding the ark. "If only Zedekiah had been faithful to God and kept his promise to Nebuchadnezzar," he wept, "all those people wouldn't be dying."

Minutes seemed like hours. Hundreds fell. Enemy soldiers scrambled through the breach, attacking the defenders from behind. Defender and invader soon met face to face on the wall, fighting hand to hand. Not a single Jew survived. A cheer rent the air as scores poured over the bridge into the helpless city.

❧❧

During the evening before the ram broke through the

wall, Zedekiah guessed his time had run out. "Jeremiah has predicted that we'll be captured," he announced to an aide, "but we're leaving tonight! And that old Babylonian lion can't stop us either." His forced confidence masked his fear.

"You're crazy," his chief general growled when Zedekiah explained his plan. "We're surrounded."

"We can do it," the king assured him, pointing to a hastily sketched map. "The enemy has heavy forces on the north and west, but only a half dozen guards by the Gate Between the Walls near Siloam. If we surprise them, we could be across the Jordan by morning."

"It might work," the general muttered, amazed at the king's newfound air of authority. "When do we start?"

"Tonight." The king smiled as he rose from his throne. "Choose your strongest men and dress them in black. This is our last chance to save the throne."

Within the hour the king's garden near the old pool teemed with life as several hundred dark-clad soldiers prepared to dash for freedom. Zedekiah and his family joined them about midnight.

Suddenly a cry rose from the direction of the Ephraim Gate: "The wall is breached! The wall is breached!"

"Let's go!" Zedekiah hissed, and the men surged toward the Gate Between the Walls.

※※

Nergalsharezer's personal servant awakened him from sound sleep. "The ram has breached the wall, my lord." He spoke in a low voice.

The general rubbed his eyes and gazed at the man who obeyed his every request. "Good. Tell my captains we'll rush the city at dawn."

About to doze off again, the young commander jerked awake as he heard footsteps pounding up the path toward his tent. Without thinking, he reached for his sword and stood.

A flutter of low, agitated voices drifted into the enclosure, and the general opened the tent flap to see what had caused all the excitement. One of the soldiers outside turned to him and spoke: "A dying guard just told me that Zedekiah and his bodyguard escaped from the city about an hour ago."

"Zedekiah?"

"Yes. They headed south along the Wadi Kidron toward the Dead Sea."

"Take a mounted brigade and catch them," the general barked to an aid who stood nearby. "I want Zedekiah alive."

❧❧

Slipping through the night, Zedekiah listened to the clip-clopping of hooves and the pounding of his own heart. The pincers of panic squeezed his chest, and he found it difficult to breathe. His head felt so filled with pressure from his terror that he feared it might explode. *I must be mad to fight against Yahweh,* he thought. *But still—still I have to run. I want to live!*

His people had died by the thousands because he had encouraged them to resist both God and Nebuchadnezzar. But *he* wanted to *live!*

The Kidron Valley seemed deserted as they stole southward. "Faster," Zedekiah whispered to his general.

The company lurched into a gallop, still cautious lest they stumble onto an enemy patrol. They longed for the light of morning and sight of the Jordan. Zedekiah often uttered encouragement to a wife or a son as they emerged from the mountains and descended to the plain that stretched toward Jericho.

Dawn climbed the sky. "Dust clouds!" a rear guard shouted. "Enemy in pursuit!"

Zedekiah whirled in his saddle, gasping at the size of the enemy forces overtaking them.

106

"Hurry!" he cried, sweeping his hand in a wide arc toward the horizon. "Ride for the Jordan!"

The men spurred their horses, but, with no prearranged plan, they galloped off in all directions at once. A few guards, his wives, and his three sons alone remained with him.

"Come back, you cowards!" Zedekiah screamed, shaking his fist. "Come back, I say!"

The dry wind blew his words back into his face, and his military escort vanished. "Let's go," he shouted, whipping his horse. But the exhausted beast—nearly dead from starvation and fatigue—had nothing more to give.

Although within sight of the Jordan, Zedekiah was captured. The Babylonians fed and gave him water, then chained him by the neck behind his captor's horse for the 20-mile trek back to Jerusalem. They did allow the king's wives to ride on horseback. "Jeremiah was right," he moaned. "If only I had listened. If only—"

After two days of forced marching, Zedekiah and his bone-weary companions gazed at the remains of their once-proud city. The stench of decaying corpses filled the air with a sweet but nauseating odor. Even his captors seemed revolted, and continued northward in search of a more suitable camping site.

Day after day Zedekiah's motley group trudged hot, rocky roads on well-blistered, unshod feet. His iron collar had chafed his neck into one large oozing sore, radiating pain throughout his body with every step. Because his elbows had been bound together behind his back, he couldn't swat the flies and other insects that feasted on his wounds.

The tortured captives, covering but eight or 10 miles a day, plodded an agonizing 18 days before reaching Nebuchadnezzar at Riblah. More than half of Zedekiah's men died, and their lifeless bodies lay abandoned to rot in the blazing sun.

Nebuchadnezzar flew into a rage when he saw Zedekiah. "You swine!" he roared. "I made you king over Judah. I gave you wealth and honor and authority. And you swore in Yahweh's name that you'd serve me *faithfully!*" He gritted his teeth. "Belteshazzar would have kept his word. Why didn't you?"

Zedekiah trembled but remained silent.

"I told you to heed Jeremiah. He warned you to surrender." Zedekiah marveled at the Babylonian ruler's knowledge of Judah's internal affairs. "But you wouldn't listen. You knew he was innocent, and still you imprisoned him. Some dispenser of justice you turned out to be!"

The Babylonian shook his fist in Zedekiah's face. "You've caused me great trouble! You've destroyed your own people. You should die!"

The executioners started toward Zedekiah, but Nebuchadnezzar waved them back and spit in Zedekiah's face. "Before I get through, you'll wish a thousand times that you *were* dead."

Nebuchadnezzar whispered to his executioner, and scowled once more at Judah's king. "Look at the results of your rebellion, Zedekiah. Executioners," he called over his shoulder, "begin your work."

Horrified, Zedekiah watched as the Babylonians forced several Jewish leaders to kneel, hands bound behind their backs, heads lowered, exposing the nape of the neck. Each executioner raised his razor-sharp sword, and, with a single stroke, severed a head from its body. One by one the leaders died: Seraiah, the chief priest (not Baruch's brother); Zephaniah, the second priest (not the prophet); three Temple doorkeepers; an army officer; five royal counselors; the chief scribe; and 60 others captured in the city.

The bloodletting numbered Zedekiah. But he cried out when they led his three sons to the death area. "No! No!" he screamed. "Not my sons!" A guard struck the king's face, and stuffed a gag into his mouth. He stared in anguish as each son knelt—and lost his head.

"Kill me! Kill me!" Zedekiah wailed as an executioner approached. *It's my turn,* he thought. *Soon it will finally be over, and peace will come—at last.*

But the Babylonian wiped his sword and shoved it into its scabbard. Then he grabbed Zedekiah's beard, and with his other forefinger he gouged out the king's eyes—first one, then the other—as the royal captive howled in pain.

"Take him to Babylon!" shouted Nebuchadnezzar. "Let him remember his retribution till the day he dies."

🌸🌿

"It's been a month since Jerusalem fell." Nebuchadnezzar chatted with the captain of his bodyguard, Nebuzaradan. Though officially titled "chief baker," the Jews called the official "chief of the butchers."

"Many people still live there." Nebuchadnezzar sat on his portable throne in Riblah. "They could rebuild their city and again become a threat. I don't like it," he sighed.

"Can I be of service, my lord?"

The two men talked for hours before the king formulated a plan. He summoned a scribe to record his decision: details on what should be done with those still living in Judah, how to dismantle the city, transportation of the captives held in the prison compound at Ramah, and other important matters.

Nebuzaradan mustered several thousand soldiers and marched to Jerusalem. He found the situation much as Nebuchadnezzar had feared: except for the breach made by the ram, and extensive minor damage, the city stood almost intact. "A well-organized warlord could rebuild Jerusalem in a matter of weeks," he told an orderly.

The Babylonians killed anyone who resisted them and rounded up everyone else for the journey to Ramah—and Babylon. Then they removed every item of value and wasted the city. They pried apart stone walls and buildings, set fire to everything wooden, including the massive cedar gates, reducing them to ashes.

Day after day the city echoed with the thump of collapsing stone and the crackle of flames devouring whatever would burn. Black smoke choked the air.

When they finished, little remained where Jerusalem had once stood. A traveler would have had difficulty getting in out of the rain. The glorious Temple of Solomon disappeared in smoke nearly 400 years after the great king dedicated it. The scarlet palace, built at such a vast expense in money and human lives, had dissolved into piles of gray-white powder.

Jerusalem was dead.

Nebuzaradan sent the loot to Babylon and headed for Ramah, where he found Jeremiah among the captives. He'd never seen a face so radiant with peace. And yet this man had spent several years caged by his own people for trying to save them from this very tragedy. *If the prophet had been king,* the Babylonian officer thought to himself, *his people would still inhabit their city.* "You're no longer a prisoner," he told Jeremiah.

"Thank you, sir. But why should I be treated so kindly? I'm but a poor slave—"

"The Great King knows how you urged Zedekiah to remain loyal," the captain interrupted, "and of all that you've suffered because of your efforts. If all your people had served Yahweh the way you and Belteshazzar have, this sad affair would never have happened."

"I've only done my duty for God. I ask no favors."

"But you shall have them." The military leader paused to read from his instructions. "The Great King, King Nebuchadnezzar of Babylon, says: 'You may go with me to Babylon, where I will provide all your needs. Or you may stay with Governor Gedaliah in Mizpah.'"

"You are kind, sir." Jeremiah bowed. "I will stay in Mizpah. I knew Gedaliah's father, and I feel safe with him."

"Very well." Nebuzaradan handed Jeremiah a sack containing small gold ingots. "This gift from the Great King should meet your needs for several months. May Yahweh, your God, bless you."

"May Yahweh bless you—and King Nebuchadnezzar."

※ ※

Judah's politics after Jerusalem's destruction remained as complicated as before. Gedaliah and his officials died in a short-lived uprising that Johanan, a Jewish military leader who had eluded the Babylonians, managed to squelch. But Johanan, thinking to save his people from Nebuchadnezzar, force-marched them to Egypt.

Johanan settled his captives in Tahpanhes, where Pharaoh maintained a palace, and before long they began to worship Egyptian gods in the neighborhood shrines.

Nebuchadnezzar, involved in plans to besiege Tyre, fumed over the continued Jewish resistance. After conquering Moab and Ammon, he marched on Egypt, defeated Pharaoh in a pitched battle, and captured Migdol, Memphis, and Tahpanhes. Rounding up the Jewish exiles, he executed most of the men and sent the survivors to Babylon in chains. No longer trusting Jewish leadership, Nebuchadnezzar put Judah under the authority of the Babylonian governor at Samaria.

"So much for them and their God," he told his chamberlain back at Riblah. "We've proved that the gods of Babylon have more power—even more than the God who rescues people from fire."

Although Nebuchadnezzar chuckled at his joke, his conscience still troubled him. An ominous foreboding lingered, warning him—lest he go too far.

Chapter 10

Cut Down the Tree

"Now that we've resolved the Judah problem," Nebuchadnezzar said to his son-in-law, "we can concentrate on Tyre."

"That city's been a thorn in our flesh for many years," Nergalsharezer replied. "But we've seriously cut into their trade."

"I'd say that we've ruined them." The older man laughed. "I've made Babylon the new center of world commerce."

"You surely have. And all but cut off their trade routes with India and other eastern nations."

The king steered the conversation back on track. "Take the army and begin the siege of Tyre at once. I'll wind up matters in Syria and Judah and join you in a few weeks."

Nestled on the Mediterranean seacoast, Tyre had been the womb of trade in the Mediterranean world for centuries. The residential area lay on the mainland, while a citadel stood offshore on a little island. It housed the palace, warehouses, arsenals, factories, and shipyards.

The citizens had become wealthy and arrogant—a law unto themselves. They believed that no force, regardless of its size, could ever conquer their island fortress.

Gate of the Gods

Ezekiel, describing their attitude, predicted the eventual fate of the city:

"The word of the Lord . . . :
'. . . to the ruler of Tyre," . . . :
In the pride of your heart
you say, 'I am a god. . . .'
But you are a man and not a god,
though you think you are as wise as a god.
Are you wiser than Daniel?
Is no secret hidden from you?
By your wisdom and understanding
you have gained wealth for yourself. . . .
And because of your wealth
your heart has grown proud. . . .

""""I am going to bring foreigners against you,
the most ruthless of nations;
they will draw their swords
against your beauty and wisdom
and pierce your shining splendor.
They will bring you down to the pit,
and you will die a violent death
in the heart of the seas."'"[1]

As the Babylonian army approached, the Tyrenians gathered in their citadel. Though crowded, they had abundant stores of food, water, weapons, and ships to obtain whatever they needed or wanted.

The mainland sections of the city fell quickly, and Nebuchadnezzar's troops rounded up every citizen who had failed to take refuge in the fortress, sending them off to Babylon in chains.

But how to besiege an island? None of the usual methods would work, as Tyre's walls extended up from foundations built upon the edge of the sea. Nebuchadnezzar couldn't construct a ramp, or use siege towers, or even get near enough to mount a stationary catapult.

Hoping to fight them with their own weapons, Nebuchadnezzar commandeered every ship, boat, and raft he could find, attempting to blockade the island. But all in vain. Babylonians knew little about ships and the sea, and found themselves no match for the veteran sailors of Tyre.

The situation became a standoff. Year after year the unbeatable Babylonian war machine exercised its well-nigh-irresistible force upon the immovable fortress of Tyre. For 13 years Nebuchadnezzar threw himself into the siege, exasperated at his failure to make a dent in the island city's defenses.

Tyre suffered in spite of its invulnerable position. The city spent enormous sums on ships and crews to bring supplies for the support of its population and defenses. Meanwhile, the prosperous trade of yesteryear continued to dwindle because of the inroads of Babylonian commerce.

Through the years the people's pride at being able to hold off the greatest army in the world began to erode because of their economic depression. The leaders of the once-prosperous city-state began to realize that they would soon be ruined. Nebuchadnezzar would never leave without taking the citadel. Something had to give if the city wanted to survive as a trading center.

So the king of Tyre called for a truce. He would submit to Nebuchadnezzar and pay a heavy tax if the city could keep its own king, while allowing a resident high commissioner to safeguard Babylon's interests.

❦❦

Never had Nebuchadnezzar seen a tree with such dense foliage and abundant fruit. It spread its branches as if to gather the whole world under its shade. He edged closer. Entire villages nestled under the tree, and numerous cattle and sheep grazed in rich meadows that extended as far as he could see.

The tree seemed to grow as he watched it. Multitudes lived within its influence. A feeling of great warmth swept over him as he realized that the tree protected and nourished all living things. Never had he felt such peace, such fulfillment, as when he gazed at the gigantic tree.

A brilliant flash from the sky startled him, and he turned to see a messenger—a holy one—standing before him. For a moment the two gazed at each other, saying nothing.

But then the messenger began to shout: "Cut down the tree and trim off its branches. Strip off its leaves and scatter its fruit. Let the animals flee from under it and the birds from its branches. But let the stump and its roots, bound with iron and bronze, remain in the ground, in the grass of the field."[2]

In horror Nebuchadnezzar watched as workers carried out the orders. But the messenger continued his announcement: "Let him be drenched with the dew of heaven, and let him live with the animals among the plants of the earth. Let his mind be changed from that of a man and let him be given the mind of an animal, till seven years pass by for him.

"The decision is announced by messengers. The holy ones declare the verdict, so that the living may know that the Most High is sovereign over the kingdoms of men and gives them to anyone he wishes and sets over them the lowliest of men."

Nebuchadnezzar opened his eyes. A dream? No—a nightmare! The vivid scenes marched through his thoughts, and he moaned as terror gripped his heart.

"What is it, my lord?" His personal servant sprang into the room.

"Ohhhh!" the king groaned. "A dream—an omen of disaster—" Swinging his feet out of bed, he sat on the edge, his head buried in his hands. "Send for my counselors—quickly!"

The servant disappeared only long enough to assign a messenger to the errand, and then returned. Pouring a goblet of wine, he tasted it to make sure it contained no poison, and then served it to the king.

Nebuchadnezzar started to drink, but handed the cup back with a sigh. "I can't shake the feeling that something horrible is about to happen—to me."

The servant helped his master dress and followed him into the little courtyard adjoining the bedroom. The king paced before a small throne near the rear wall and accepted the second glass of wine his servant pushed at him. He glanced, impatient, at the doorway waiting for his counselors.

Nebuchadnezzar felt more depressed than ever. His counselors couldn't interpret his dream. This one had been different from the image dream he'd had more than 30 years before, because this time he remembered all the details. But even with that help, his "divinely inspired" wise men had been unable to decipher its meaning.

"Belteshazzar!" The king smiled as Daniel bowed. "I'm so glad that you've come. No mystery is too difficult for you."

Carefully Nebuchadnezzar related the dream to Daniel: the tree, how it blessed all living things, his happiness in its presence, the messenger, the loss of the tree, the metal bands, the seven-year prediction, the animal heart, and the power of the Most High to govern all humanity.

"This is the dream, Belteshazzar, and none of the wise men can interpret it. But you can, for the spirit of the holy gods is in you."

Daniel's smile had disappeared as the king related his dream. Alarmed at what he heard, he seemed unable to speak.

"Belteshazzar, don't let the dream or its meaning alarm you."

"My lord"—Daniel's voice sounded hoarse—"if only the dream applied to your enemies!"

An expression of sadness clouded his face and tears collected in the corners of his eyes. "The tree you saw," he continued, "which grew large and strong, with its top touching the sky, visible to the whole earth, with beautiful leaves and abundant fruit, providing food for all, giving shelter to the beasts of the field, and having nesting places in its branches for the birds of the air—" Daniel almost choked on the next words. "You, O king, are that tree! You have become great and strong; your greatness has grown until it reaches the sky, and your dominion extends to distant parts of the earth.

"You, O king, saw a messenger, a holy one, coming down from heaven and saying, 'Cut down the tree . . . leave the stump . . . in the grass of the field. . . . Let him be drenched with the dew . . . ; let him live like the wild animals, until seven times pass by for him.'"

Tears streamed down Daniel's face. "This is the interpretation, O king, and this is the decree the Most High has issued against my lord the king: You will be driven away from people and will live with the wild animals; you will eat grass like cattle and be drenched with the dew of heaven. Seven years will pass by for you until you acknowledge that the Most High is sovereign over the kingdoms of men and gives them to anyone he wishes. The command to leave the stump of the tree with its roots means that your kingdom will be restored to you when you acknowledge that Heaven rules."

Suddenly drained, Daniel fell on his knees before Nebuchadnezzar. His eyes searched those of his master as he pleaded with him. "Therefore, O king, be pleased to accept my advice: Renounce your sins by doing what is right, and your wickedness by being kind to the oppressed. It may be that then your prosperity will continue."

Daniel knew that the fulfillment of divine predictions, whether good or evil, often depended upon the reaction of the one who received the message. All God's promises and threats are conditional. If the heart changes, then the promise, or the curse, alters as well.[3]

"O king," Daniel repeated. "If you repent of your sins, turn to God, and serve Him faithfully, this terrible thing need never happen." Lowering his gaze, he wiped away his tears with a corner of his robe. Then he rose and left the courtyard.

The king sat quietly for a long time, visibly shaken, thinking about the events of the past few hours.

Belteshazzar must really care, to risk his life like that, he thought. *And he's right. I have been wicked. I should repent. And if I do—if I do, then all the horrible events I saw in the dream will never happen.*

"I'll do it," he said aloud.

The chamberlain looked up, startled.

"I'll follow Belteshazzar's counsel." He smiled. "They'll never cut down this tree."

For many weeks the tree dream haunted Nebuchadnezzar. Deep within his mind he knew that Daniel told the truth, that he would suffer the terrible penalty of the dream if he strayed from his commitment to Yahweh, God of the Jews.

But keeping such a decision proved difficult in pagan Babylon. Spiritual commitment itself found no resistance among the overreligious Babylonians, who worshipped many gods. But Nebuchadnezzar had chosen to ally himself with one God—excluding all others—and the God of a subjugated people at that.

Most Babylonians knew that Daniel and his three high-ranking friends belonged to this "one-god" cult. And many religious leaders blamed them for the heresy Nebuchadnezzar included in his edicts from time to time.

Gate of the Gods

Everyone believed in dreams, of course. But few liked Daniel's interpretation of the tree dream. They couldn't understand why the supreme counselor had rebuked the king—even though it may have been needed. And why had the king accepted the reproof without executing Daniel? And why still had he committed himself to worship a God who gave such unpopular dreams?

Before long Nebuchadnezzar began again to reflect the attitudes of his servants, and the warning of Daniel wore thin. Soon the king no longer remembered his commitment to Yahweh.

Through the years he had subdued his enemies and had spent much time planning and building. During times of peace he had strengthened and beautified his capital, fulfilling his passion to make Babylon the greatest city in the world. It had bolstered pride in his city—and in himself.

Among his triumphs stood the hanging gardens, built for his wife—the lovely Amuhia, daughter of the king of Media—to remind her of the flowered hills of home. The terraced structure sat in the northeast angle of the palace near the Ishtar Gate.

He had also built a series of irrigation canals to make better use of the Euphrates River. This system included an immense artificial basin, about 40 feet deep, to collect excess water during spring rains for use during dry spells later in the year. The desert plains of Shinar had become a grain basket for much of the region.

And he had not forgotten his gods. During his reign he built more than 50 temples, more than 900 sanctuaries and nearly 400 street altars.

While beautifying the city, the king had also strengthened its defenses. He nearly doubled the length of the walls, while adding a second, outer wall with towers every 55 yards.

All these structures had walls consisting of a mud-brick

core, covered with an outer layer of glazed, fired bricks. Many of the walls were yellow, the gate areas sky-blue, the palaces rose colored, and the temples white.

Throughout the city few buildings or walls or streets existed that had not been in some way affected by the building plans of Nebuchadnezzar.

※※

A year had passed since the king's tree dream. One day Nebuchadnezzar led a group of visiting royalty on a tour of his glorious city, and after a spectacular circuit they returned to the southern palace. They emerged onto a second-story balcony overlooking the hanging gardens, with the temple tower soaring above them less than a half mile away. The king, overcome by the splendor, called for a scribe to record his thoughts. Filled with the pride of personal accomplishment and surrounded by the great men of his realm, he waxed eloquent.

"I, Nebuchadnezzar, have made Babylon, the holy city, the glory of the great gods, more prominent than before, and have promoted its rebuilding. I have caused the sanctuaries of gods and goddesses to lighten up like the day. No king among all kings has ever created, no earlier king has ever built, what I have magnificently built for Marduk. I have furthered to the utmost the equipment of Esagila [Marduk's temple], and the renovation of Babylon more than had ever been done before. . . . May the way of my life be long, may I rejoice in offspring, may my offspring rule over the black-headed people into all eternity, and may the mentioning of my name be proclaimed for good at all future times."[4]

Nebuchadnezzar's guests began to applaud the well-phrased tribute to the greatest king who ever—

A thunderclap startled them.

The day had been clear, sunny, and hot. Thunderstorms

were extremely rare. They frightened the people of the desert plains.

But this thunderclap brought no rain. It rolled on for more than a minute, vibrating the foundations of the city. The king's guests staggered about, knocked almost senseless by the ear-breaking volume. They leaned against walls and railings. Some fell on their faces, grasping the floor to find stability amidst their gyrating world.

Nebuchadnezzar dropped to his knees, glancing from side to side, his arms lifted as if to shield himself from an unseen attacker. But to him, it was no thunder. It was a voice from heaven pronouncing his doom.

"This is what is decreed for you, King Nebuchadnezzar: Your royal authority has been taken from you. You will be driven away from people and will live with the wild animals; you will eat grass like cattle. Seven times will pass by for you until you acknowledge that the Most High is sovereign over the kingdoms of men and gives them to anyone he wishes."[5]

Nebuchadnezzar's eyes began to glaze. The superior intelligence with which he had governed his great empire faded into unreachable corners of his brain. He stumbled forward on hands and knees, uttering guttural sounds. Saliva dribbled from the corners of his mouth, and within minutes his well-groomed beard became matted with spit and dust.

The king's attendants shrank back in terror. The crawling, dribbling ruler gazed about him. He recognized every person, saw the loathing with which they regarded him, and heard every word they spoke, but he had no control over his actions. Although a part of him wanted to speak, to say that he could still think, and plan, and manage the empire's business, his voice produced only grunts.

Crawling toward one of his guests, a personal friend, he pleaded for help. But the man retreated in terror. Before long they had abandoned him—everyone except his personal bodyguards. And even they kept their distance.

Seeking someone to help him, he entered the palace and tried to summon his personal servants as he went. But his growls and grunts, his expression, and his uncontrollable grimaces frightened everyone away.

Finally Nebuchadnezzar dragged himself outside into the garden that he had designed. The grass and well-tended flowers created a strange hunger that gnawed at his insides. He tried to contain it, to control his actions. But he couldn't. The greatest king in the world squatted in the courtyard of his palace, pulling up grass and stuffing it into his mouth, munching it as though he were an ox.

Daniel hurried to the palace. He had long prayed that Nebuchadnezzar would remember the warning that God had given him in the tree dream. But pride had gained control of the ruler's heart, and now the worst had happened.

Entering the palace garden, Daniel saw Nebuchadnezzar grazing on the lawn. Approaching closer, he bowed with courtesy.

At last, Nebuchadnezzar thought. *Belteshazzar will understand. He'll help me.*

But the king was unable to control his behavior. Instead of asking for help, he made a vicious growl and lunged at his friend.

Daniel had to back off. "O king," he pleaded. "It's me, Belteshazzar. Let me help you."

But Nebuchadnezzar responded with another life-threatening attack that forced Daniel to leave the garden.

"The palace physicians have been unable to cure him," a servant explained to him later. "We've summoned a famous Egyptian sorcerer who specializes in treating madness. But he's traveling abroad, and it may take weeks for him to return."

"And when he returns," Daniel replied, glancing back at the garden, "he, too, will find that he can do nothing."

"Nothing, my lord?"

"Nothing. You see, this is a judgment from Yahweh, God of heaven and earth. It will last for seven years, and we cannot stop it. It will have to run its course."

"Run its course?" The chamberlain had joined them.

"Don't fear, lord chamberlain. The king's guards will protect him. And you know how the people regard madness—they think he's possessed by supernatural spirits. They'll fear that any harm done to him, or any attempt to take his throne, will bring a curse down upon the one responsible for the injustice."

"So we let him roam the palace gardens and see that he's unmolested?"

"Exactly."

"But what about the kingdom?"

"You know the king well, what he'd do under every circumstance." He paused, putting his finger to his lips, knowing the amount of authority he took upon himself. "You must run the empire—just as he would were he still in charge. You carry out his plans and maintain the kingdom for him. When the seven-year curse has passed, Nebuchadnezzar will rule once more. God has decreed it—it will come to pass."

Several times a week Daniel visited the courtyard, looking for signs of Nebuchadnezzar's return to sanity. While the divine decree had said "seven years," yet he knew that God often withdrew His judgments when the person repented. And he hoped that the king would humble himself and receive healing.

From time to time Daniel took along the king's personal servant. With the help of the guards, they cornered the royal maniac, bound him, and cleaned him up—cutting his hair, beard, and nails—to spare him the misery of infestation from fleas and lice.

❦❦

Nebuchadnezzar remained aware of his surroundings throughout the period of his insanity, and yet he couldn't interact with them. In the beginning he blamed his predicament on Daniel, and would have killed the man had he been able to control his limbs.

As the years rolled by, his bitterness ebbed into depression, and he lost all concern for either the present or the future. His past greatness seemed but a vapor that had appeared for a moment, then vanished forever.

But in time despair gave way to acceptance. He came to realize that he couldn't change his condition, and he gave up fighting it. While outwardly he seemed as insane as before, peace reigned within his heart. Gradually he began to appreciate the warmth of the sun and the coolness of the grass—even its flavor no longer irritated him. Delighting in the many colors of the flowers in his courtyard, he came to covet the gentle treatment of Daniel and his allies among the palace servants.

As he thought about his reign—his triumphs, trials, dreams, and the people he'd known—he marveled at the stupidity and arrogance of the Jewish kings: Jehoiakim, Jehoiachin, Zedekiah, and their false prophets. Their treachery had filled him with fury.

But he had allowed their pettiness to blind him to something far more important: Many Jews served Yahweh faithfully—Daniel, Jeremiah, Shadrach, Meshach, and Abednego. They stood as prime examples of true people of God. Now he realized that instead of fretting over the bad, he should have concentrated on the good.

Gate of the Gods

If only I'd seen that before, he berated himself. *If only I'd trusted God, and listened to Belteshazzar—I wouldn't be here now. And yet—and yet without this madness,* he thought, *I wouldn't have discovered the personal power of God in my own life.*

O Lord God of heaven and earth—the unspoken cry came from the mind of a king the world thought insane, a prayer from the depths of a soul longing for peace and joy. *O Lord God, forgive me my foolish pride. Bless me even as You've blessed Belteshazzar.*

No thought of healing. No thought of regaining the throne. Just a simple prayer for forgiveness—for blessing.

A soft warmth radiated through Nebuchadnezzar's body, a vibrancy that he hadn't known for years. His legs and arms tingled with life. Without thinking, he rose to his feet.

Turning his face toward the sky, he spoke his first words in seven years—a prayer: "Thanks be to Yahweh for His marvelous gifts."

At that instant Daniel entered the garden on his daily visit. His heart seemed to leap into his throat when he saw Nebuchadnezzar standing, his face gazing toward the sky, speaking words of thanksgiving.

"My lord!" The Hebrew official bounded across the lawn.

"Belteshazzar!" The king caught his friend in a powerful embrace. "Oh, how much I've wanted to thank you for your kind and loving care all these years."

"It was nothing, my lord." Tears streaked down Daniel's cheeks as he looked into a face that once again sparkled with intelligence.

The guards who lounged on a nearby bench leaped to their feet in fright, as Daniel and the once-mad king strode toward them. But they relaxed when they saw the all-but-forgotten luster in Nebuchadnezzar's eyes and a friendly smile on his lips.

One of them raced into the palace to spread the news,

while the others surrounded him, and—forgetting their position—hugged their king. Nebuchadnezzar had been healed.

※※

Babylon rejoiced at the return of Nebuchadnezzar the magnificent. And yet, he seemed to be different. He had the same energy, the same love of justice, the same insistence on quality workmanship as before. But instead of exalting himself, he proclaimed his newfound faith in the God who created all things.

Soon after his return to the throne Nebuchadnezzar asked Daniel to help him write an edict explaining how his pride had led to humiliation, and revealing his joyous acceptance of a new divine Master.

"At the end of [my seven years of madness], I, Nebuchadnezzar, raised my eyes toward heaven, and my sanity was restored. Then I praised the Most High; I honored and glorified him who lives forever.

"His dominion is an eternal dominion;
  his kingdom endures from generation to generation.
  All the peoples of the earth
  are regarded as nothing.
  He does as he pleases
  with the powers of heaven
  and the peoples of the earth.
  No one can hold back his hand
  or say to him: 'What have you done?'

"At the same time that my sanity was restored, my honor and splendor were returned to me for the glory of my kingdom. My advisers and nobles sought me out, and I was restored to my throne and became even greater than before. Now I, Nebuchadnezzar, praise and exalt and glorify the

Gate of the Gods

King of heaven, because everything he does is right and all his ways are just. And those who walk in pride he is able to humble."[6]

---

[1] Ezekial 28:1-8
[2] Much of the dialogue in this section comes from Daniel 4.
[3] See Ezekiel 33:14-16.
[4] From an actual inscription, now housed in the Berlin Museum.
[5] Daniel 4:31,32.
[6] Verses 34-37.